STATE OF THE HEART

STATE OF THE HEART
Brett Walpole

THE ACT…

THE SCENE…

THE FRAME…

www.BUBBLEFLIGHT.com

TITLES

"Acting is a masochistic form of exhibitionism. It is not quite the occupation of an adult."
- Laurence Olivier

"Art is the means by which we communicate what it feels like to be alive."
- Antony Gormley

"I looked through a lens and ended up abandoning everything else."
- Sebastião Salgado

"I went to buy some camouflage trousers the other day but I couldn't find any."
- Tommy Cooper

EXT. LONDON PUBLIC SPACES - MORNING

A young man, CARL LLOYD-BROOKS (29), wearing a grey all-in-one boiler suit spattered with paint, takes photographs in the great pulsing city of London as he listens to music on large orange headphones. At first Carl is seen close up, then a slow zoom out from a very high vantage point, reveals him to be a lonely speck in the densely populated metropolis.

> CARL (V/O)
> I didn't start out in life with a plan to be an artist, I just sort of fell into it. Recently though, I've been feeling an intense desire to change my status, to be a more authentic version of who I seem to have become. The problem is, for anyone looking, I've already achieved the ideal of personal freedom. I'm lucky, I do what I want, when I want, but something's not quiet right.

INT. CARL'S ART STUDIO, HOXTON - DAY

Carl arrives home and closes all the curtains in this large warehouse space furnished with leather sofas and strewn all about with creative chaos. The room is thrown into darkness.

> CARL (V/O)
> You see from my point of view I'm hopelessly trapped. All I want is to be the author of my own new, original story-line, I want to break free from what I can only describe as a self-imposed solitary confinement.

He attaches his camera to a projector and an image of the London sky-line appears on a large canvass. Rolling up his sleeves he begins drawing on the canvass.

4

CARL (V/O)

Tonight is a big night, and the success or failure of the restructuring of my way of life depends on it. I want it to be the beginning of a complete change in my lifestyle, my work practices and my attitude in general. However, it's very clear to me that I'll be needing the kind of help which I'm simply unable to imagine.

EXT. "CASA NUEVA" FINE ART GALLERY, CHELSEA - NIGHT

A small art gallery, illuminated well inside, displays Carl's paintings in it's large windows. A buzz of people can be seen within as more visitors arrive and enter through the tall sliding glass doors.

INT. "CASA NUEVA" FINE ART GALLERY, CHELSEA - NIGHT

The atmospheric music inside is Jazz which can be heard behind the murmur of thirty or so guests. They are of many types, by turns creatively and wealthily dressed. Hung on the walls are large paintings of London, all clearly works by Carl in variations of his style. Carl is wearing a suit and tie and is flanked by CHLOE DE LA ROSA (56) and MILAN VAN DER BERG (59), both impeccably dressed. Around them are gathered several would-be buyers, drinking glasses of Champagne, who listen intently. Chloe speaks in a Spanish accent.

CHLOE

When we discovered him, I kept on saying, Carl, will you promise me that you will just keep painting!

Milan talks with a Dutch accent.

MILAN

That was only three months ago, this man works fast, and already these works are selling just as fast, so buy whilst you can!

Carl is softly spoken and quite humble.

CARL

The truth is, my process allows me to focus on both the detail *and* the broad strokes. London is perfect in that regard, it's so wide ranging in the scale of its identity.

At this moment SUZIE RICHARDS (23), who is pretty and slightly shy, walks up carrying a tray of full Champagne glasses.

CHLOE

Oh Suzie, there you are.

Chloe takes a drink from the tray.

CARL

I see Chloe has you working overtime Suzie, I hope you're being paid appropriately.

SUZIE

It's the least I can do. Does anyone need a refill?

MILAN

In fact it's Suzie here we have to thank for bringing Carl to our attention. It's a lovely story of chance really. Suzie's flatmate, Iris is with Sebastian, an old art school friend of Carl's.

6

                                SUZIE

That's right. In fact I've just seen them over there
together, and it looks like they're in need of a drink.
Excuse me.

Suzie walks over to SEBASTIAN McEWAN (30), a tall and strong
man, and IRIS SWIFT (25), who is considerably shorter and dressed in
bright clothes.

                                IRIS

Hey Suze, how's it going?

                                SUZIE

Very well, I think, from all the little red dots going up
by the paintings, half have been sold already!

                             SEBASTIAN

What about Carl, how's he handling the pressure and
all these money types?

                                SUZIE

I don't know, he seems in his element I guess. Chloe
and Milan are just parading him around like a prize
race-horse.

                             SEBASTIAN

He'll be ok as long as he doesn't drink too much or
start flirting with the employees.

Suzie looks away embarrassed. Iris notices.

                                IRIS

Am I missing something here? You and the star of the
show? Really and in the workplace too, I'm shocked.

SUZIE

Iris! There's nothing there really.

A JAPANESE WOMAN is talking with Carl.

JAPANESE WOMAN

So, Mr. Lloyd Brooks, please can you tell me how you
would describe your own work with these beautiful
paintings.

CARL

I begin with photographs, I've developed a whole way
of looking at London with longer lenses, then I use
these images as reference for the paintings. I suppose
if you have to label them, they're photo-realistic in
nature. The crucial aspect is to ensure…

At this moment Carl looks up to see ROBIN TUCKER (28) enter the
gallery, his gaze is taken by her. She is beautiful and elegant with an
immediate presence and some sex appeal, several people turn as she
enters.

CARL

…the original… images have the utmost… beauty and
integrity…

Robin sees Sebastian and walks towards him.

CARL

Would you excuse me for a moment.

Carl walks towards the trio of Iris, Sebastian and Robin. As he reaches
them Robin looks up.

8

ROBIN

Carl, is that you? I hardly recognised you in a suit.

CARL

Robin! You look great, how are you?

ROBIN

Well, I'm very well.

SEBASTIAN

And famous, don't forget famous.

ROBIN

I'm not famous.

SEBASTIAN

Not quite yet, girl, but soon.

CARL

How, did you, how did you know to come?

ROBIN

I walked by the other day and I saw this little, what
would you call it, 'happening', advertised. You've made
it. You always said you could, that you would, now
you really have.

CARL

And you, all grown up, career on the up and up. Seb
and I have followed your rise from a distance. It's
stupid that we've grown out of touch.

                    ROBIN
Now's the perfect time to start sorting that out.

Suzie, who has been circulating, arrives with her tray of Champagne glasses, Robin takes one.

                    ROBIN
Thank you.

                    CARL
Oh, Robin this is Suzie, she works here, she helped organise all of this, she and Iris share a flat together.

                    ROBIN
You've done a splendid job Suzie, make this phoney old art student look like a professional.

                    SUZIE
It's a pleasure, Carl is the talk of the town right now. Are you, are you Robin Tucker?

Robin laughs.

                    ROBIN
Yes, that I am, live and direct.

                    SUZIE
I love you. I mean I love all your films.

                    ROBIN
Thank you, I've only done two. Wait 'til you see the latest one though, it's a real stinker. Director from Spain thought he was Picasso, it's going to be a proper lemon. You heard it here first.

SUZIE

Carl never told me he knew you.

ROBIN

Carl and I and Seb here were at art school together, back in the day. Seb got into advertising, I went into show biz and it looks like Carl here's the only one who didn't sell out, kept the torch alight for fine art.

CARL

We had a lot of fun together.

Chloe comes up to the group.

CHLOE

Carl dear, sorry, can I borrow you for a moment, there's some people over here with money burning a hole in their pockets.

Carl turns away.

CARL

I'll catch you guys in a bit.

Carl and Chloe disappear into the crowded room.

ROBIN

You know, I knew he'd go all the way with it, but where does he go from here?

SEBASTIAN

Robin, before I forget, let me give you my card.

                    ROBIN
    Oh, here, have one of mine too.

They exchange business cards. Iris who has been in the background
chirps up.

                    IRIS
    Can I have one. I'm Iris, Sebastian's significant other.

                    SEBASTIAN
    I'm sorry honey. Robin this is Iris, we're together,
    we're working together too at the moment, on a pizza
    commercial. Iris makes puppets.

                    ROBIN
    Hi Iris. Puppets, that's fascinating.

                    IRIS
    It sure is, everyone's a puppet, you just can't always see
    the strings.

Robin gives Iris her business card.

                    IRIS
    Thank you.

Iris reads the business card carefully.

                    IRIS
    So you're an actor then...

Time passes as the people in the studio mingle and jostle together and
paintings are sold. The Champagne is consumed and the empty bottles

line up on a table to one side where Suzie works hard. Carl is engaged in another sales-related conversation when Suzie walks by again. Carl catches her.

CARL

Hey, Suze, can I get another drink?

SUZIE

Sure, here you go. If you need me for anything else...

Robin walks up to the two of them.

ROBIN

Carl, old bean, I've got to split. I'm meeting with Rufus Ronson tomorrow, early morning.

CARL

Rufus Ronson, wow! I've actually heard of him. That's a move up isn't it?

ROBIN

Apparently he wants me in his new movie. It could be my breakthrough to the States.

CARL

Do you have to go? I wanted to talk some more.

ROBIN

Here's my card, call me, anytime.

Carl takes the card and looks at it.

CARL

Great I'll call, we've got a lot of catching up to do.

ROBIN

You're right about that, a lot of water under the bridge
since we were last shaking the world up.

CARL

Yep, time just keeps going.

ROBIN

I'm going, you will call right?

CARL

I'll call, I'll definitely call.

ROBIN

Good-bye Suzie, great to meet you, congratulations on
tonight. Bye, painter dude.

Robin kisses him on the cheek, turns and leaves. Carl drinks his drink
down in one and takes another from Suzie's tray.

SUZIE

She's amazing.

CARL

Yep, she's pretty cool alright.

CHLOE

Suzie, over here a minute please.

Suzie walks over towards Chloe. Carl is left looking at one of his own
paintings for a moment. Milan walks up to him.

MILAN

So Carl my boy. This is a big success tonight, no?

CARL

Yes, success!

He drinks more. Milan moves closer to him and leans in.

MILAN

Let me tell you. This, all this, this isn't success.

Carl looks at him.

CARL

No?

MILAN

No. Not at all, this is just... a moment in your life.
Even tomorrow it will be gone like that glass of
Champagne. In fact you are not even here, not right
now. What you are feeling, experiencing, is a mirage.

CARL

It feels pretty real.

MILAN

No. You are not real, it is why you do not know who
you are. You are going to have to face reality and ask
the one question that matters most.

CARL

What is that?

15

Carl is now entranced at the Dutch man looking him in the eyes. Milan moves his face even closer to Carl's and talks in a deep, low whisper as the sounds of people in the gallery are muted.

                    MILAN
          Who is Carl Lloyd-Brooks?

Carl is in a state of bemused shock.

                    MILAN
          Look deep within to find the answer.

Milan immediately turns and walks away leaving Carl staring at one of his own paintings. Suzie glides past and sees him gazing. Once again staring at the painting Carl seems to be the only one motionless. As the evening continues, people come and go speeded up in time and move all around him as though he is at once the most important person there and also forgotten. Eventually the room is all but empty. Chloe talks to him, lifting him from his introspection.

                    CHLOE
Carl darling, what an unbelievable success, you must be over the moon? Carl?

                    CARL
          Er.. yes. Have you seen Milan?

                    CHLOE
No, he's gone, he had to catch a flight back to Amsterdam. You should go now too. If you wait a moment Suzie can come with you, you can walk to the tube together. I thought she might give you some ideas for further work, she's a clever girl you know.

                         CARL

    That's a good idea.

                         CHLOE

    Suzie!

Carl waits a few moments. Suzie puts her coat on and they drift out of
the gallery, through the sliding glass doors, and into the deep London
night.

EXT. "CASA NUEVA" FINE ART GALLERY, CHELSEA - NIGHT

They walk in silence at first.

EXT. LONDON STREETS - NIGHT

As Carl walks with Suzie it is clear he is a little drunk. He stumbles.

                         SUZIE

Hey there sailor, are you ok?

                         CARL

Oh, I'll be fine, just you see. Let's just sit down for a little while shall
we.

Carl sits on a nearby bench, Suzie sits next to him. She is a little shy
but clearly likes Carl.

                         SUZIE

    Are you happy Carl?

17

CARL

Happy? Of course I'm happy.

SUZIE

I mean in life, without being drunk.

CARL

Yeah, other people make me happy. You make me
happy Suzie, you're funny and cute and, a bit odd.

SUZIE

That's very kind, I think, I just thought maybe tonight
that you were sort of, distant. It was your big night.

CARL

I suppose I usually find a way to make things look
easier than they are. I'm a natural in that sense.

SUZIE

You can always talk to me, you know, about whatever,
Art stuff if you like. Chloe thought I might be able to
help, with ideas for future work. You know I've got a
degree in all that.

CARL

Suzie, you are smart, you are beautiful and you are
kind too. But   are you happy?

SUZIE

I don't know, how do you really know if you are.

CARL

I know how you know.

Carl steals a kiss from Suzie, who seems to be aware of what's going on but enjoys the moment all the same.

                    CARL
        That's how you know.

                    SUZIE
        You are drunk Mr. Lloyd-Brooks. I think you might
        not make it home via the tube. Why don't we get you a
        taxi.

                    CARL
        Excellent idea.

Suzie stands and quickly hails a taxi. She helps Carl open the door and he gets in. Before he goes he gives Suzie his business card.

                    CARL
        Can you call me tomorrow Suzie, just to talk? I'd like
        to talk with you when I'm in charge of myself. Will
        you call?

                    SUZIE
        Yes, I'll call you tomorrow, make sure the package has
        reached it's destination.

The taxi pulls away and Carl waves, shouting out the window as he does so.

                    CARL
        Thank you Suzie! You're the business!

Suzie flicks the business card in her hands and mutters to herself.

                            SUZIE
    I wish I was.

INT. TAXI CAB - NIGHT

As the taxi speeds through the night-time city lights, Carl tries to wake
himself up. At one point the taxi driver swerves sharply and beeps his
horn.

                          TAXI DRIVER
          Bloody idiot, get off the road! Sorry about that sir,
          moped drivers think they own the place this time of
          night.

Carl sits upright but with his eyes closed. In a kind of trance, the words
of Milan suddenly come back to him in a bass-tone, resonant whisper
that fills Carl's head.

                          MILAN (V/O)
          This is just a moment in your life. You are not even
          here. Who is Carl Lloyd-Brooks?

Carl opens his eyes and whispers to himself.

                            CARL
          Who is Carl Lloyd-Brooks?

Then he says out loud.

                            CARL
          Who is Carl Lloyd-Brooks?

                    TAXI DRIVER
Sorry sir, what was that?

                       CARL
Er... No, nothing, I was just thinking out loud.

                    TAXI DRIVER
I do that all the time. You think cabbies like talking to
their fares, it's 'cos we're actually always just talking to
ourselves. I bet you wouldn't believe what most
cabbies say when they're just driving around on their
own, make a good movie that, you know about a taxi
driver, and what he says and does and thinks about,
what he gets up to when he's not driving his cab...

The taxi driver's voice trails off and goes quiet as Carl slumps and falls
asleep.

INT. RUFUS RONSON'S LONDON HOTEL SUITE - MORNING

The American RUFUS RONSON (38), is eating a pastry, sitting on a
chaise lounge in a fairly ornate hotel apartment with high ceilings and
light streaming through large windows, where fine net curtains blow in
and out on the breeze. There is a knock on the door. Rufus shouts out,
a mouthful of food obscuring a broad Californian accent.

                       RUFUS
             Come in, come in!

Robin walks in through the door, a vision of elegance and calm.

                         21

ROBIN

Hello, Mr Ronson. I'm sorry I'm a few minutes late, there was a problem with…

RUFUS

Oh don't worry about anything. My god, you look great, do you always look that great? It's like you're in a movie or something.

Rufus stands up and walks half way across the large room, wiping his hands on a serviette and extending his hand to Robin. They shake hands.

RUFUS

Come and sit down, you must have some of these Danish pastries, they're to die for.

They walk over and sit down, Robin on a chair by the chaise lounge. She takes off her coat.

RUFUS

Check out the coffee too, they have everything in this place. The studio is taking care of the check, so you can order anything you like, some eggs Benedict perhaps?

ROBIN

Thank you, that's very kind, I've just started a diet, and I'm still in that phase where I'm sticking to it.

RUFUS

Oh. OK. Business then, Look, I've got to tell you Robin, you've got the part, that's a fact, that's in the bag. I love your work to date and I hear your latest flick is a surefire winner, a work of art so I heard it said. So this, this is just a formality really, I'm still playing around with some of the characters and I just wanted to try something with you. There's this piece, the monologue at the climax that I'm just, well, I'm in two minds about it. Do you think you could read it for me?

Rufus hands across a few pieces of paper to Robin.

ROBIN

I know the monologue, I can do it from memory if you like?

RUFUS

You can! Well, that's great. In your own time then.

Robin composes herself, rolling up her sleeves and taking off her glasses. She takes a long time to move herself subtly into a deep inner place. Holding herself in a dignified pose she holds onto one of the net curtains which continues to blow in the breeze. Rufus is already transfixed, before she begins, as he holds a pastry in his motionless hand. As Robin travels through the monologue, the sounds of the traffic outside the window die to a muted blur, and the atmosphere in the hotel room is electric with tension.

ROBIN

The foul look of his contorted face as though he'd had the last laugh. The unnatural way his broken limbs were twisted and gnarly like the roots of a tree. No-one would shed a tear for him, or his like, and I couldn't help but wonder if this was his last mark on the world he'd left behind. Was his journey over now, or was he merely handing the baton over to me? I already knew

one of his secrets, now I had to carry his legacy
towards another world, a world where dead men speak
and the living have to listen. I'd heard his voice and it
had put the chill in me. It was fearful cold running
through my very soul and I vowed never to go that
place again.

Robin finishes and for a few seconds Rufus remains motionless,
eventually Robin breaks the silence and stillness.

                    ROBIN
Was that OK? I mean I can go with less intensity, you
know more throw away…

                    RUFUS
Er no! Just remember this, I want you to do it exactly
the same on the day. I'm really, that was… Wow.

                    ROBIN
Thanks, I was thinking maybe with an American
accent, or maybe Irish, I wasn't sure what you had in
mind for her, it er, wasn't clear.

                    RUFUS
Well, I'll get back to you on that. There has been a
development though I wanted to fly by you. It's
regards the male lead, I believe you know him, Martin
Stevens?

                    ROBIN
Martin? Oh yes, we go back to art school, in fact we
kind of kicked off our acting careers together.

RUFUS

Well, I heard that you had some history, I did a little
research you know, and I thought maybe there was
some chemistry there… Something that might add to
the on-screen… fizz.

Robin becomes slightly defensive but still entirely in control of her
behaviour.

ROBIN

Oh, well Mr. Ronson, I'm sure I can't let you into any
secrets that may or may not have had their origins at
that time. Let's just say that Martin and I are well
aware of each other's talents, strengths and weaknesses
that kind of thing, if that's what you're interested in.

Rufus becomes quite animated and a little excited too.

RUFUS

That's it! That's it exactly! This is going to be a
fiendishly dynamic feeling, I know it. Now Robin, I
can't be here for a while. I have to shoot back Stateside
for a to work the Production wheels, but I have
Martin's number here, he's expecting a call from you,
to discuss the story. Maybe you could get into
character a little, start the ball rolling so to speak, in the
next few days would be good.

Rufus hands over a business card to Robin who takes it.

RUFUS

Are you sure you won't have some of these? A
croissant perhaps? I'm sure they won't mind if you
take a few away with you.

ROBIN

Thank you but no. I'll certainly give Martin a call. I must say I'm fascinated to be working with you, your methodology has started to create quite a stir this side of the Atlantic.

RUFUS

Well, really it's only based on a set of arbitrary rules I've picked up along the way but I've been getting some interesting feedbacks as to the results it's true. Robin, it's been damn fine meeting you at last, it's going to be magic. I'll get my people to talk to your people about all the small print and we'll be making waves before you can say Stanislavski.

Robin stands and they shake hands.

ROBIN

Thank you Mr. Ronson. I hope I can live up to expectations.

RUFUS

You will, I'm so sure about this, and from now on it's just Rufus.

ROBIN

Goodbye, Rufus. Enjoy London whilst you're here.

RUFUS

Bye.

Rufus resumes his coffee and pastry as though nothing has happened. Robin leaves, picking up a serviette from a trolley in the corridor and wiping her hands with it before throwing it away.

INT. CARL'S STUDIO - DAY

Carl is lying in bed, he rolls over and looks at his old fashioned bell-ringer clock, it's 2pm. In the open plan studio there are various 'zones' rather than individual rooms. He gets up slowly, takes a shower and then putting on a dressing gown and walking into a kitchen area, makes coffee. He is pouring his coffee and eating a croissant when the phone rings, it's Suzie.

INT. SUZIE AND IRIS' FLAT - DAY

Iris is sitting on a sofa, sewing together a puppet for the pizza commercial. Suzie sits on a small veranda outside, smoking a cigarette whilst she talks with Carl on the phone.

> SUZIE
> Hi Carl, it's Suzie, how are you doing?

> CARL
> Oh, I'll live. Listen, thanks for pushing me into that cab last night.

> SUZIE
> That's ok, all part of the gallery's service, you know, looking after it's assets.

> CARL
> I don't feel too much like an asset.

> SUZIE
> You realise how successful last night was though don't you? We sold all but three pieces. That's unheard of.

CARL

It's amazing what people will part with cash for these days. I don't know where they get their money.

SUZIE

Does it matter?

CARL

No, no it doesn't I suppose. It'll be good to get a big fat cheque from Chloe, that's the truth, after she's taken her healthy cut of course. Hey does this mean I'm partly responsible for paying your wages?

SUZIE

I'm an integral link in the chain of supply and demand.

CARL

That you are indeed, in deed.

SUZIE

Listen, I was wondering whether you wanted to grab some lunch or something, if you haven't already eaten.

CARL

Ah, no, I haven't eaten, not properly yet, I've actually only just got up. Why don't you come over here for a bit? I mean if you'd like to check out the splendour in which the great artist lives.

SUZIE

Ooh, sounds good, see where the magic happens.

                    CARL
    I can't promise any magic, but I can make you a coffee.

                    SUZIE
    That's great, I'd love to. How about in a couple of
    hours or so?

                    CARL
    Perfect, give me time to do some dusting.

                    SUZIE
    Hah! Ok, see you then.

                    CARL
    See ya Suzie.

They hang up.
                    IRIS
    What did he say?

                    SUZIE
    I'm going to go visit him, at his studio.

                    IRIS
    Ooo. Lucky you, not even I have been allowed into the
    inner sanctum.

                    SUZIE
    What shall I wear?

                    IRIS
    Go rustic, dungarees and wellies.

INT. CARL'S STUDIO - AFTERNOON

Music plays from Carl's Hi-Fi as he tidies. There is a buzz, he walks to the door, opens it and greets Suzie, who looks serene and casual.

                              SUZIE
     Hi!

                              CARL
          Suzie, welcome to my world! Come in, come in.

Suzie walks in carrying a small box.

                              SUZIE
          I brought Sushi.

                              CARL
          Ah, brilliant, I love Sushi.

Suzie looks around at the large space. She is overwhelmed by the place and walks freely throughout.

                              SUZIE
          Wow, it's incredible, how do you afford all this? It must
          cost you a small fortune.

                              CARL
          Ah well there's the thing. Rent is a shocker but. You
          see I came into some money when I was twenty-one.
          After college, and a few disastrous attempts at living a
          normal life, I found this place.

                              SUZIE
          How long have you had it?

                            CARL

This is year four. Truth be told the inheritance has all
but gone so last night's sales will be a real life saver.

                            SUZIE

I love it.

                            CARL

Shall we eat?

                            SUZIE

Yep, good idea.

Carl gets some glasses of water and they sit on a large leather sofa to
eat the Sushi. As they eat Suzie is polite but curious.

                            SUZIE

So what is your direction now? I mean with your painting.

                            CARL

Ah, you know it's tricky. That series last night, the city
skylines, you don't want to know what that was like.
Taking the photos was superb, I love being out and
about but the paintings... Eventually I was just
knocking them out like a production line, it was quite
demoralising actually. It's great just to be rid of them.

                            SUZIE

It's quite a gift just to be able to make so many, so
quickly.

CARL

I don't know. It was the monotony that got to me. I had
to go in to some kind of zen trance. It seems like a bad
dream now.

SUZIE

People seem to like them, I like them.

CARL

Yeah, popularity and integrity don't always go hand in
hand though do they? Milan said something to me, I
can't quite remember the exact words right now but it
was along the lines of, 'Is this you?' and you know, I
just don't know if I can answer that.

SUZIE

Mmm, tricky. What's next then?

CARL

This is it, I have no idea, none whatsoever, I'm just
floating in the wind, looking for some place to land.
How about you Suzie? You're just always flitting

around in the background, Chloe always has you doing
something, what's your thing?

SUZIE

I got the job, about four months ago and…

CARL

No, not the job, I mean you, what's going on with you,
yourself? Tell me something.

Suzie is a little awkward being put on the spot as it's obvious she looks up to Carl.

                              SUZIE
          I'm... It was funny meeting your friend Robin Tucker
          last night because, well I've been thinking about doing
          some acting, try to…

                              CARL
          Don't do it! Come on you've got a great job, why be an
          actor?

                              SUZIE
          I realised last night seeing Robin up close, for real and
          especially in the gallery that she, acting in general, its
          the art of life, and I want to be living it.

Suzie grows in confidence a little as she talks about this.

                              CARL
          I've got every respect for that I have, really. I mean I
          can't act, I've always known that.

                              SUZIE
          Have you ever tried?

                              CARL
          Believe me it would not be pretty! Robin makes it look
          so easy, so effortless but... I know someone else too, I
          met him through Robin years ago, a man by the name
          of Martin Stevens.

Suzie flips.

                    SUZIE
You know Martin Stevens! I think he's amazing. He's
like a god, or a Demi-god at least, what's he like, in
person?

                    CARL
Honestly, I think he's a bit of a dick. He certainly
fancies himself. I mean he is a good actor but... I'm not
sure he's such a good person. Maybe you'll meet him
one day, make up your own mind.

                    SUZIE
That would be so cool.

                    CARL
Yeah, it's all very cool... Robin is a different story, you
know she was a painter too once.

                    SUZIE
I want to hear all of it…

Carl and Suzie carry on talking, Carl gets a bottle of wine, and then as
the light starts to fade, another. He closes the many curtains in the
studio, turning on several atmospheric lights as he does so. The music
changes. They begin kissing on the sofa.

INT. CARL'S STUDIO - NIGHT

It is now the middle of the night. Carl is in bed with Suzie who has
fallen asleep. He is wide awake, and looks at Suzie. The moonlight
streaming through a gap in the curtains falls across her face, bare
shoulders and long hair, which lays across the duvet and pillow. She
appears blissful and beautiful.

INT. CARL'S STUIO - MORNING

The couple lie in peace as the sun now throws beams of light across them. Suzie is the first to stir, it's early. On a bedside table is a miniature camera, she reaches out and picks it up, looking closely at its functions. She has obviously learned photography and quietly composes a shot of Carl as lies asleep. With the 'click' Carl wakes and smiles.

                              CARL
          Good morning. You're not the press are you?

                              SUZIE
          I love this little camera, it's so cute and funky.

                              CARL
          Yeah I've had it ages, it's a bit of a toy really.

With a groan, Carl leans over the side of his bed and reaches out to a large professional camera which hangs on a hook.

                              CARL
          This is what I use for work, it's all singing all dancing.
          Really good quality, I love this thing.

After playing around with it for a while and sitting up in bed he points his camera at Suzie and they both take photos of each other taking a photo.

                              CARL
          I think you'd call that a shoot out.

                              SUZIE
          Your gun's bigger than mine!

CARL

And I'm quick on the draw.

Carl moves and takes another photo of her. As he does so he begins to get absorbed by the activity, standing up in just his boxer shorts and shooting from other angles. Suzie is barely covered by the sheets as he photographs her as she shoots with the little camera. Becoming more involved he climbs up a short ladder to a small mezzanine level and takes pictures from ten feet or so up, directly above the bed.

CARL

You know if you change your mind about acting you'd make a seriously good model.

SUZIE

Be quiet! I'm serious about the acting thing you know.

CARL

I know. I think you should start going to acting classes.

SUZIE

You think that's the best bet?

All this time Carl is taking more photographs.

CARL

Definitely, see if you like it, if not I can keep you here as my muse.

SUZIE

I'm not sure I'm qualified...

CARL

Oh, you're qualified alright. What happens if you, just kind of, throw the duvet to one side?

SUZIE

You're terrible... You mean like this?

We do not see the naked form of Suzie but Carl is clearly smitten on both a personal and artistic level.

CARL

You look beautiful from up here Suzie.

SUZIE

Only from up there?

CARL

The whole picture is pretty amazing if you ask me.

SUZIE

Do you ever consider the moral implications of your line of work?

CARL

Er. I'm the same as most people, ethics are kind of a distraction.

SUZIE

What is this anyway, work or play? Weren't you ever told not to mix business with pleasure?

CARL

I'm er.. just preparing you for the kind of situation you might find yourself in an acting role.

                    SUZIE
I don't think this is acting.

                    CARL
Can you tell me the difference between acting and
normal behaviour, I've never understood that.

                    SUZIE
Are you telling me you think this is normal?

Carl stops photographing, and climbs down the ladder.

                    CARL
You're right, perhaps it isn't but then who makes up the
rules for artists?

                    SUZIE
No-one, that's the problem... I'm going to make some
coffee.

Suzie gets up and puts on her clothes then disappears to the kitchen.
Carl reviews the images on his camera, looking almost shocked at what
he has captured.

                CARL (To himself)
        That's hot!

As he gets dressed Robin's business card falls out of his trousers, he
picks it up, and looks at it. Milan's words come back to him in his
mind.

                    MILAN (V/O)
Who is Carl Lloyd-Brooks?

Carl looks up to the ceiling, places the card in his wallet and finishes getting dressed. He walks to the kitchen.

CARL

Suzie, if you want to act you definitely should, just do it. I reckon you could find a night class or a weekend course you can fit around you job at the gallery.

SUZIE

I'm going to, you watch, you'll see a whole different side of me. Once I get the bit between my teeth I'm a totally different animal.

CARL

My god, what kind of animal are you at the moment?

SUZIE

Dangerous, early morning, in need of a coffee animal that has to be gone in a just a few minutes.

CARL

Oh, ok, I thought we could do something.

SUZIE

No, I told Iris I'd help her with a few things and then Chloe's got me working overtime, wrapping up and packaging your paintings for delivery.

CARL

Oh, well thank you for that.

SUZIE

All part of the wonderful and weird world of fine art. Here's your coffee.

Suzie hands him his coffee and gets the rest of her things, drinks some of her coffee quickly, kisses Carl and is out of the door before Carl can take a breath.

                    SUZIE
        I've got to fly, I'll call soon… Bye!

When she is gone, Carl drinks his coffee and is standing in slight shock.

                    CARL (To himself)
        Wow, that was something else!

Wandering around he eventually comes across his camera, he puts his coffee down and looks at the images again. He hooks it up to his projector, the curtains are still all drawn, and he projects one image of Suzie partly naked onto the huge brick wall at one end of the studio. He takes a very large bare canvass, hangs it in the centre on the wall and resizes and refocuses the image to fit. It's a beautiful shot from directly above the bed. Playing some music on his Hi-Fi, and with the image partly covering his own body, he begins to draw in pencil on the canvass.

INT. SEBASTIAN'S APARTMENT - DAY

In a large office at his home Sebastian sits with Iris behind a large, tilted drawing desk upon which are the storyboards for the tv commercial that they are working on. The pictures are hand drawn, in colour and are already at quite an advanced stage.

                    IRIS
        I'm not so sure this is the right message, it's too long.

                    SEBASTIAN
We could cut these two and that would leave us with
the voice over starting here and ending here.

                      IRIS
I prefer that.

                    SEBASTIAN
Then I think we're done. I'll get this to the Director this
afternoon.

                      IRIS
Seb...

                    SEBASTIAN
What is it?

                      IRIS
Do you think Carl is serious about Suze? It's just you
know him better than I do and, well she's sort of a bit...
vulnerable.

Sebastian rolls up the story boards and puts them in a tube.

                    SEBASTIAN
Oh, yeah, I know what you mean. He's a good sort
really, he won't harm her, they're probably just having
a lot of fun together. It's good to see that. At college,
with him and Robin, it was painful to watch.

                      IRIS
They ended up hurting each other?

SEBASTIAN

No, it was a 'will they, won't' they saga that lasted for two years, and as far as I know they never... did, if you get me.

IRIS

I'd kind of had this image of them in some tumultuous, artistic relationship that was full of triumph and tragedy and produced great works of incredible art.

SEBASTIAN

I think that's what they thought they had going, fact is it was all just a load of pretentious hot air.

IRIS

That's a bit of a disappointment.

SEBASTIAN

I may be wrong, maybe they were you know, doing it, all the time, may be they had something very special whatever it was, but it was very secretive, as far as I could see.

Sebastian then becomes less casual and more serious.

SEBASTIAN (CONT.)

Then his father died and Robin dropped out to become an actress and, well the good times came to an end. He graduated though, I was proud of him for that.

IRIS

That's so sad, his dad died.

SEBASTIAN

They were really close too which made it worse,
afterwards, and he got left all this money, and he didn't
cope with that very well either. I had to pick up the
pieces. But he got the studio, after a lot of deviations,
and now look at him, our boy's a success.

IRIS

Suzie never stops going on about him, it's getting a bit
much actually. We've got acting class tonight, I'll get
yet another dose of just how incredible he is.

SEBASTIAN

How's the class going?

IRIS

I've learned almost everything about nothing. I mean,
last week the teacher had us sitting on chairs, wailing
and screaming, for half an hour. She wouldn't let us
stop until each one of us was crying. But it's fun and
it's all for Suze really, she wants it so much, she puts
her whole self into it, the preparation, the passion, the
performance. It's very inspiring the drive she has.

SEBASTIAN

Do you want coffee?

IRIS

No, let's have sex instead.

SEBASTIAN

Alright then.

INT. ACTING CLASS ROOM - EVENING

Suzie and Iris are sitting together at their acting class, with ELEANOR (39), the tutor, and eight or so other students. Suzie gets up and is standing opposite FREDDY (20), a young man with long hair. They are close to each other and taking it in turns to make animal noises, increasing in volume.

                    SUZIE
        Woof! Woof! Ruff! Ruff!

                    FREDDY
    Moo!

Suzie then slaps Freddy hard across the face.

                    ELEANOR
        Good, good! How did that feel for you Suzie?

                    SUZIE
    Liberating.

                    ELEANOR
        How about you Freddy, how did it feel?

Freddy is rubbing his cheek which has come up red.

                    FREDDY
    Real!

All the group except Freddy laugh.

ELEANOR

Ok, so we've learned that in order to act, react and interact we must, on some fundamental level be talking the same language and that this language does not have to be a spoken language. All dramatic tension comes from our ability or inability to do this. The meaning of the intention in acting is carried within our body language, and it is this which is universal. Thank you Freddy and Suzie. Nice slap Suzie, good action.

SUZIE

Thank you Eleanor.

Suzie returns to her seat next to Iris.

ELEANOR

Ok, now we're warmed up, hopeful as warm as Freddy's face, let's tackle our scenes. Remember, forget the dialogue as it's written for now, I just want you to get across the point of the scene. Find the beats and communicate them. This is about crucial moments linked together to make us feel our way through the essence of the narrative. Iris is whispering to Suzie.

IRIS

I've only learned the dialogue, I thought we were just supposed to learn the dialogue!

SUZIE

Oh, Iris! Don't use the dialogue. We'll just have to wing it, follow me, improvise.

IRIS

Improvise!

45

                    SUZIE
Just make it up as you go along…

                    ELEANOR
Suzie, Iris. Step up, I believe you've chosen a scene
from the Alfred Hitchcock film "Vertigo". Take the
stage, this should be interesting….

They stand up and walk to the stage. Iris pulls up a chair and climbs up
onto it, standing above Suzie.

                    ELEANOR
OK, in your own time.

Iris coughs, the group is quiet, Iris pauses before speaking.

                    IRIS
I'm scared and I want to get down.

The group laugh but Suzie is embarrassed.

                    SUZIE
Iris!

                    ELEANOR
Stop right there. Fantastic! I loved it! Ok who's next?

INT. CHLOE'S OFFICE, GALLERY - DAY

Chloe calls Carl who answers.

                    46

CHLOE

Carl honey, I want you to listen. All the paintings have
sold. Yes, it's true, I know it's wonderful. I'll have your
money to you asap. Yes, as we discussed. The only
problem is now I have bare walls and that's not a
situation that can continue. I need new work and I
need it soon. It's good you've finished one but one
isn't good enough, I need a series, series sell. Ok, be in
touch soon. Ciao.

INT. CARL'S STUDIO - DAY

Carl hangs up. He is standing in front of the large, finished painting of
the nude of Suzie nude, in bed from above.

CARL

Genius!

INT. ROBIN'S AGENT'S OFFICE - DAY

Robin walks into her agent's office. Her agent, CHARLIE STAFFORD
(40) is sitting behind a large desk an is surrounded by full book shelves,
stacks of screenplays and various computers, printers, fax machines and
a photo-copier.

CHARLIE

Robin, come in, come in, take a seat. You look
wonderful, you really do.

ROBIN

Thank you Charlie, I love your ear-rings.

CHARLIE

Oh, a little gift from Spielberg when he was in town a few years ago. Listen, it's all very exciting. I have the Rufus Ronson contract right here.

Charlie holds up a piece of paper.

ROBIN

Wow, that was quick, where do I sign?

CHARLIE

Here's the thing, there's some clauses in it I'm not sure about, mainly to do with insurance and overtime, things like that. It's an American contract and they're always, well, different. I want the legal department to take a good look at it first if that's ok with you?

ROBIN

Certainly, whatever you think best.

CHARLIE

This is the big one Robin.

ROBIN

I know, I'm super excited. The script is great, I love his work, this is going to be the springboard to the US and to be honest I'll be breaking out of the, 'Robin Tucker' stereotype.

CHARLIE

Yes, I was never quite sure why you took that chocolate commercial, the one with the diamonds and the tiger. It was just... funny, not in a good way. Just... wrong.

ROBIN

Oh it was just a bit of fun, and it paid well.

CHARLIE

Alright, we could discuss the merits of television
advertising all day but for now we've got to
concentrate on the bigger picture. The question of
developing your career in the right direction young
lady. I'll get back to you with   details as they emerge.

ROBIN

Ok, is that it? Are we all good?

CHARLIE

Don't go anywhere until this is all signed and sealed.

ROBIN

Roger that.

CHARLIE

Wonderful.

Robin gets up and goes towards the door.

ROBIN

Bye then.

CHARLIE

Bye Robin.

Robin closes the door behind her.

CHARLIE

Really, tigers *and* diamonds.

49

INT. CARL'S STUDIO - DAY

There is a fresh canvass on the far wall. Carl is just covering up the
finished painting with a large sheet, there are several others, also
finished which he covers cup as well with more sheets. Music plays in
the studio, and sprawled around the two large sofas is Suzie, Iris and
five of the students from the acting class. They dominate the space
with laughter and antics. Carl is moving around frustrated. Eventually
he joins them and puts an arm around Suzie.

                    CARL
        You guys seem to be very lively.

                    SUZIE
        It's free expression, you should try it.

Suzie shrugs off Carl's arm.
                    SUZIE
        There's some more beers in the fridge, could you bring
        a few?

Carl fetches the beers from the kitchen and returns. He gives them to
one of the students.

                    STUDENT
        Thanks Carl old buddy.

The student cracks open the beer which explodes and sprays beer all
over the place, including some on Carl which he brushes off.

                    STUDENT 1
        Sorry about that man, looks like you gave me a live
        one! Next one's on me!

                    CARL
    Don't worry about it. Do you guys mind if I take a few
    photos. I won't get in your way.

Another student reaches for a beer.

                  STUDENT 2
    Hey go ahead and shoot dude, good practice, we all
    need exposure to the media!

Carl picks up his camera from nearby and starts taking shots at first
from a distance then moving closer and closer to the group. The still
photos are shown in black and white as he takes them. The closer in he
moves the more cinematic the shots become with two shots, over the
shoulder shots, close ups and extreme close ups. Carl loses himself in
the photography and the music, until he is close to Suzie and she stops
him.

                   SUZIE
    You can get too close you know, it kind of detracts
    from the natural moment.

Carl stops and says nothing but reviews his photos.

                   SUZIE
    You know what we need honey, we need a party. This
    place would be perfect for a real kick ass party.

                  STUDENT 2
    Party! Yeah, this place needs more people, fill it with
    funky folk and some real tunes.

                    CARL
    I don't know, I've got work I have to do and…

SUZIE

Come on Carl, you'd enjoy it. It'd be break for you.
You don't get out much so why not bring it all here.

CARL

Something small would be ok, I guess.

SUZIE

All our friends could meet each other. You could invite
Robin Tucker and Martin Stevens.

STUDENT 1

Yeah, do it Carl Meister. Party!

The rest of the group start hollering and shouting until Carl can really
only say yes.

CARL

Ok, Ok, Let's have a proper, full on party! Next
Saturday!

The group cheer Carl's name and begin a frenzied activity on their
phones. Carl walks away with his camera and sees Iris who is by the
Hi-Fi looking at records.

CARL

They're like animals!

IRIS

I know, fortunately they're not in the wild, it's just a
zoo.

CARL

In my studio!

                              IRIS

It's ok, they're all limited by their self imposed social
structure. There are rules for them.

                              CARL

I don't see the rules.

                              IRIS

That's the puppets with invisible strings thing,
someone's controlling them.

                              CARL

It certainly isn't me.
                              IRIS

They only behave like that because they have to
believe they've already made it. It's sort of beautiful
really, all totally delusional but for them they're just
behaving normally.

One of the students does a back flip off of the sofa.

                              CARL

Normal for a zoo maybe.

                              IRIS

So you're having a party then, am I invited?

                              CARL

For sure, I'll need someone to keep me sane.

                              IRIS

Sanity's over-rated. Wait til you start seeing the strings
and find yourself attaching symbolic meaning to them.
Are you going to invite Robin?

                               53

CARL

I've got to think about that, we have... some history
together.

IRIS

Ah, history's over-rated too. You want to take a leaf out
of their book. Get into the now.

Iris gestures towards the group who are piling on top of each other in a
mess of bodies.

IRIS

Maybe not now, now.

CARL

I'll give Seb a call.

IRIS

Smart move.

Carl walks out of the studio.

EXT. CARL'S STUDIO - DAY

Carl sits on the fire-escape outside his door and calls Sebastian.

CARL

Hi Seb, are you busy?

INT. SEBASTIAN'S CAR - DAY

Sebastian is driving his car through the city, listening to music when the
phone rings, he answers.

54

SEBASTIAN

Carl, no, I'm just driving to a meeting at a production
company. What can I do for you?

CARL

It seems like there's going to be a party, at mine, this
Saturday. Are you free?

SEBASTIAN

Yep, sure am. A party, excellent, everything can happen
at a party.

CARL

Do you think I should invite Robin?

SEBASTIAN

Of course, you should. You've got her number haven't
you?

CARL

Yeah, I've got it.

SEBASTIAN

Even if she can't come, it'll give you a chance to talk,
god knows you two were always good at that.

CARL

Ok, I'll call, what about Martin, Suzie really wants to
meet him, she's got a thing about him.

SEBASTIAN

I know they guy's a spanner but he'll give the night that
show biz shine that everyone get's off on. Yeah, call
him up. Hey is Iris with you?

                              CARL
Yes, she is, do you want a word with her?

                           SEBASTIAN
No, just tell her the storyboards were approved by the
director.

                              CARL
OK, will do. Thanks Seb.

                           SEBASTIAN
Laters my friend.

                              CARL
See ya.

EXT. CARL'S STUDIO - DAY

Carl removes Robin's business card from his wallet and studies it. As
he paces around outside Milan's voice comes into his head.

                           MILAN (V/O)
Who is Carl Lloyd-Brooks?

Carl dials her number and she answers.

EXT. COVENT GARDEN - DAY

Robin is walking along the street carrying a couple of shopping bags.
She is upbeat, carefree and happy.

                    ROBIN
Hello.

                    CARL
Hi Robin, it's Carl.

                    ROBIN
Carl! Great to hear your voice. You took your time, I
thought you might have forgotten me.

                    CARL
No Robin, I don't forget about you, and that's the truth.

                    ROBIN
Ah, that's nice but hey, let's not get into some deep and
meaningful about what happened and what didn't
happen in days gone by. I'm sure we've both moved on.

                    CARL
You have, it was out of this world to see you at the
gallery. It was like you were just the same but it was
hard not to see your image had just exploded.

                    ROBIN
I am just the same, it's just I've got this job that makes
me seem unreal or something.

                    CARL
That front you had, you've kind of worked on it,
developed it makes you appear... detached.

ROBIN

You of all people know there's stuff behind that. I'm still just me.

CARL

You're right, we can have this conversation another time. I've actually got a question for you.

ROBIN

As long as its not about that chocolate commercial I did.

CARL

Ah, yes, that may have been a bit of a mistake. No, do you want to come to a party at mine on Saturday?

ROBIN

Love to.

CARL

Cool, I'll send you the location. I was going to ask Martin too, what do you think?

ROBIN

If you have to.

CARL

It's just Suzie's mad about him.

ROBIN

Is that Suzie who works at the gallery.

CARL

Yep, that's her.

ROBIN

Are you and her... together?

CARL

Kind of. It's complicated, I think she thinks I'm
something I'm not.

ROBIN

I get that all the time. I might be able to bring
someone with me actually, a sort of surprise guest.

CARL

Mmm, sounds intriguing. Ok, I guess I'll see you
Saturday.

ROBIN

I'll look forward to it, and Carl, don't sweat the small
stuff, right.

CARL

I hear you, bye Robin.

ROBIN

Cheers tiger.

She hangs up.

EXT. CARL'S STUDIO - DAY

Carl hangs up, and talks to himself, whilst walking to another area of
the space where he dials.

                              CARL
That wasn't so hard. Now for Mr. Martin Stevens,
successful and handsome heart-throb ham, originally
from Hounslow.

He calls, and Martin answers.

INT. HEALTH SPA - DAY

MARTIN STEVENS (32), who has movie-star good looks and perfect
hair, is having a back massage. His phone rings, he looks at it and
answers. The female masseur continues the massage.

                             MARTIN
Carl you old devil, how the hell are you?

                              CARL
I think I'm doing ok, just had a big exhibition.

                             MARTIN
Ah, and how is that famous talent of yours. Are you
still knocking out masterpieces in record time?

                              CARL
Umm, I'm sort of trying to head in a different direction
currently, it's difficult, it's hard to explain.

                             MARTIN
Hard, I'm sure it is. Listen I'm kind of tied up right
now, can we make this snappy?

CARL

Er, yes. I just wondered if you wanted to come to a
party at mine on Saturday. Sebastian will be there and
Robin too.

MARTIN

Ah, I assume you're talking about Miss Tucker. I
suppose she told you we are most likely to be working
together in the very near future.

CARL

No, she didn't mention it.

MARTIN

The new Rufus Ronson picture, we're starring opposite
each other.

CARL

That's cool, I guess. It would be great to hear all about
it on Saturday.

MARTIN

I can't promise anything, I'm a very busy man, but if I
show, you'll know.

CARL

Thanks Martin, I hope you can make it.

MARTIN

So long, Carl.

CARL

Cheers Martin. Bye.

They hang up. Martin's massage continues.

> MARTIN
> That's it, can you go up a bit?

INT. CARL'S STUDIO - NIGHT

The party is in full swing. The whole space is transformed from empty and static to packed and dynamic. A Dj spins records and a gold disco ball fleetingly illuminates the faces of the guests. Some people are drinking and talking others are dancing. Almost everyone is there; Milan and Chloe, Eleanor, Martin, Carl and Suzie and all the acting students and their friends make up the bulk of the people.

Carl is talking to VINCE (23) the Dj when Robin arrives nearby with the American Rufus Ronson, who is dressed in black, she sees Carl and they walk up to him.

> ROBIN
> Carl!

> CARL
> Robin! You made it.

> ROBIN
> Carl I'd like you to meet Mr. Rufus Ronson.

> CARL
> Bloody hell! Mr. Ronson, pleased to meet you,
> welcome to the party!

They shake hands.

                              RUFUS

Hi Carl, just Rufus, please. Robin has told me all
about you, I hear you're shaking things up in the art
world.

                              CARL

To be honest with you Rufus, I'm kind of stuck at the
moment, not sure what I'm up to or who I am for that
matter!

                              RUFUS

I get you, a little identity crisis is a good thing every
now and then believe me.

                              CARL

Do you guys want some drinks? There's everything
over there.

                              ROBIN

We'll talk later.

                              CARL

Definitely.

Rufus and Robin go in search of drinks. Suzie has been watching them
from a slight distance and walks up to Carl with a drink in her hand.

                              SUZIE

Was that Rufus Ronson with Robin?

                              CARL

Yeah, crazy heh!

SUZIE

You didn't say he was going to be here.

CARL

I had no idea, a 'mystery guest'. You should talk to
him, might not ever get another opportunity.

SUZIE

Oh I'll talk to him.

CARL

You know Martin Stevens is here, I saw him about ten
minutes ago.

SUZIE

I've just been with him, he's just the same as he is in
the movies.

CARL

Yeah watch out for him Suze, he's a sly old devil.

SUZIE

I've sussed him out already. Where's Robin?

Sebastian and Iris arrive carrying a huge tower of perhaps ten large
pizza boxes which they take towards kitchen. Sebastian then walks to
Vince, the Dj who takes off his headphones to listen to him. As
Sebastian walks away Vince picks up a mike, brings the levels down on
the music and speaks.

VINCE

Hear me now! There is a magnitude of free pizza,
representing every flavour under the sun in the kitchen
at this very moment in time. Advisory is to consume

whilst hot. This has been a public service broadcast, now back to the tunes.

Robin comes back on her own to Carl who is still with Suzie. Robin ignores Suzie and talks straight to Carl. Suzie just gazes at Robin.

                    ROBIN
Hey, I directed Rufus to Martin, they'll have lots to talk about.

                    CARL
I heard you and Martin are going to be working together.

                    ROBIN
Did Martin tell you that?

                    CARL
Yeah.

                    ROBIN
It's not all signed and sealed as of yet, but I think it's a pretty sure thing.

                    CARL
Looks like Seb's scored a winner with the pizzas.

                    ROBIN
I'll be getting some of that soon, I'm famished. Hey are you ok, I mean all this, public gatherings never used to be your thing.

                    CARL
I'm a bit disorientated seeing this is my home. I don't know half the people here.

Suzie who has been standing quietly to one side, tentatively takes a pause in Carl and Robin's conversation, to speak.

SUZIE

Robin, do you think we could have a chat later, sort of professional acting stuff?

ROBIN

Of course, of course.

SUZIE

Thank you so much. I'm just going over there, I won't be a minute.

CARL

Ok Suze.

Suzie walks away.

ROBIN

But you're doing ok, in general?

CARL

I'm not sure what's going on with me, since the exhibition I've been... totally lost and trying not to show it.

Suzie walks towards Rufus Ronson and Martin who are standing to one side drinking. She passes Chloe and Milan who are talking together.

CHLOE

It all appears to be chaos from where I'm standing.

MILAN

It's simply the spirit of youth Chloe. These young souls
are just reaching out to delineate their boundaries.

CHLOE

But must they be such hedonists. I fear young Carl
should be setting his sights a little higher, than this
"pop culture", he'll waste his talent, you mark my
words.

MILAN

I sensed he has a certain, what shall I call it, a certain
unease regarding his status in the world. It occurs to
me that is like so many artists, dislocated from his true
place in society.

CHLOE

Oh, really don't talk nonsense. The boy's a painter, it's
what he does, and he's good at it.

MILAN

Is he? Does he have that essence which will mark him
out as a unique voice, or is he just popular?

CHLOE

His work sells.

MILAN

So do ready cooked meals.

Eleanor through the crowd of people who is sitting in a corner drinking
and talking to a small number of her students. They are surrounding her
and listening intently.

ELEANOR

This is your world, this is where the acting brain is at home. You need to stop, absorb every moment, every movement. Really SEE the subtext of this situation.

Suddenly another one of the students runs over to the group.

STUDENT

Hey, Rufus Ronson is here! Apparently he's on the look out for extras for a new movie, now, right now!

All the students run off leaving Eleanor sitting on her own. She picks up a can of lager and drinks.

ELEANOR

Extras!

Suzie is with Rufus Ronson and Martin, she is speaking in a different way, more refined with a kind of class that was perhaps hidden before.

SUZIE

I am new to this, it's true, however my signature style is such that a fresh take, a clean new attitude, unaffected and uncomplicated by the conventions of modern acting means I am a fresh, albeit raw new talent.

RUFUS

Suzie, I hear you and the funny thing is, your look and your philosophy are exactly what I've leaning towards recently. Here's what I'm going to do. This is my office number, call tomorrow and I'm going to personally find you something.

68

Rufus hands Suzie his business card.

                    SUZIE
        Thank you, I'm most grateful and the chance to work
        with the delicious Mr. Stevens here just gives me
        goosebumps.

                    RUFUS
        It's a pleasure, you really do have that look Suzie.

At that moment some of the students arrive, one of the bolder of whom
addresses Rufus.

                    STUDENT
        Mr. Ronson, we hear you're looking for extras.

                    RUFUS
        Yes, yes, call this number tomorrow!

Rufus is fairly swamped as he hands out business cards to the groups of
students.

                    RUFUS
        That's it I've run out!

                    SUZIE
        Would you excuse us Mr. Ronson, you seem to have
        your work cut out.

                    RUFUS
        Certainly, come back to rescue me though!

SUZIE

Oh you're in your element Rufus. Martin would you
like to accompany me to find another drink? I have so
many questions to ask you.

MARTIN

Ok, fire away, what do you want to know?

They walk off together.

SUZIE

What's the secret to professional success?

MARTIN

Oh, that's easy, you have to submit to the process
completely, mind, body and soul. I can tell you, when I
first started out there was no such thing as networking,
you had to have a resume and photographs, all that
kind of thing. You say you're in art, I'm a collector
myself. My god, you do look beautiful in the dress...

Robin and Carl are in his portioned off sleeping area, the sound of the
party continues but Carl is getting a bit stressed.

CARL

I have no idea what this party is for.

ROBIN

People are having fun, just chill out, will you.

CARL

I'm not having fun, and apparently this is my party.

Robin moves close to him and holds him by his hand.

ROBIN

Hey, I'm here, there's a reason to smile, don't you
think?

CARL

It's good to see you, it's amazing actually but it's all a
bit much, I was fine before I saw you last, then, all this
has happened and you're here. I just wish everyone
would go home and it would be just you and me,
watching tv or something.

ROBIN

Do you want to go outside for a bit?

CARL

That's a great idea.

They get their coats and leave the studio. As they are walking towards
the door Suzie stops them.

SUZIE

Ah, Robin, I was wondering whether we could have
that chat?

ROBIN

Sorry, not now Suzie, maybe later.

Carl and Suzie leave together, with Suzie left looking slightly
menaced. Freddy the student walks up to Eleanor who is still sitting in
the same place as before but is alone and drinking. He approaches her.

ELEANOR

Oh, Hi Jamie, don't you want to go and get a role as an
extra with the others. You do know the Ronson
brothers are here.

FREDDY

It's Freddy. No, I'm more interested in becoming a real
actor. That's if you think acting can truly be taught. Do
you think you can teach me how to act?

Eleanor looks dejected and takes another swig of her beer. She looks at
Jamie up and down.

ELEANOR

Probably not.

FREDDY

I was thinking, do you feel like getting a bit naughty
instead? I've found a bed just around there.

He points. Eleanor looks at him in disbelief and then eyes him up and
down.

ELEANOR

Just around there you say?

Martin and Suzie are in an embrace and kissing in a far corner. They
come up for air.

MARTIN

I thought you and Carl were sort of together.

SUZIE

I think he's started making other plans. Right now,
you're the only man I'm interested in.

MARTIN

It's important to feel that you're the centre of attention
sometimes.

Carl and Robin come back into the studio.

CARL

I'm just going to find Suzie, I think I ought to make
things clear.

ROBIN

OK, I'll be right here.

Carl walks around the party then spots Suzie and Martin, locked
together in a passionate kiss. He stares for a good while then smiles to
himself before walking away. As he does so, Milan stops him in dead
in his tracks and once again gets his face close to Carl's.

CARL

Milan, I…

MILAN

Who is Carl Lloyd-Brooks?

CARL

I, er, no... I don't know.

MILAN

Look within yourself at the areas of your life where
struggle, conflict and suffering reside and reflect that
upon your canvass.

Carl is understandably slightly intimidated by the larger man.

CARL

I can do that.

MILAN

Can you? My gallery in Amsterdam is currently in a
position to be buying works from London, Chloe and I
are in close collaboration. I have seen your work and it
is good, but simply put, it is not good enough, not yet.

CARL

I can improve and am beginning to have some new
ideas…

MILAN

Be silent. If you have the inner strength to feed your
talents you will go far, but if you cannot mine the caves
of your soul you will end up as nothing but a puppet,
on an island, surrounded by a sea of chaos, controlled
by anyone who feels so inclined. Now work!

Milan turns and leaves disappearing into the slowly dwindle number of
people. Carl is left stunned and remains so until Robin comes to his
aid.

ROBIN

Are you alright? Who was that?

                              CARL

That was Milan.

                             ROBIN

What did he want?

                              CARL

…Work.

The party continues with people mixing freely. The drink disappears
and then, moment by moment, in the early hours, one by one and in
couples, people say their goodbyes and leave. With one last song
coming to an end and the DJ being the very last to leave, the main area
of the studio is left in a state of disarray and completely vacated. The
gold disco ball continues to rotate and it is just Robin and Carl together
as it rotates silently above them. Robin puts her arms around Carl's
shoulders and they kiss.

INT. CARL'S STUDIO - MORNING

Carl wakes with Robin beside him in his bed. He smiles and relaxes
completely. Soon Robin wakes too as the sunlight comes through the
window and falls across her face. She sees Carl looking at her and
mumbles into her pillow.

                             ROBIN

What are you looking at?

Carl laughs a little.

                              CARL

A movie star.

                               75

ROBIN

Oh please. I bet I look like a hundred bucks.

CARL

You look... natural.

ROBIN

Natural what?

She wakes up fully and sits up in bed.

CARL

I realise there's something I've never told you before.

ROBIN

Don't tell me, you were a Cub Scout.

Carl laughs.

CARL

Actually I was but... At college, day three of the first
year I switched from photography to fine art, just so
that I could be in your class.

ROBIN

Seriously? I didn't think we met until the second year.

CARL

Yeah, well you were always looking... elsewhere.

ROBIN

I liked you. You didn't speak to me for about six
months.

CARL

I was shy.

ROBIN

Shy! We didn't know who we were back then.

CARL

You did! As soon as you started your acting extra
curricular activities you were away. I couldn't reach
you.

ROBIN

Really, that's how it was? You know I chose acting,
Seb chose the advertising game, but you didn't really
choose did you?

CARL

No, I got left trying to do the one thing that I was
basically no good at. I'm an improver.

ROBIN

And you've done it all this time. Man, that's tragic.
The past needn't hold you back. You realise, you can
still change, you can still choose.

CARL

I was thinking about that, what would you think if I
was to say I was considering a career in acting?

ROBIN

Stop right there, that's not even funny.

CARL

I was just messing around.

ROBIN

Shit, what time is it?

Robin looks at his big bedside clock.

CARL

It's ten thirty.

ROBIN

Fuck! I've got a meeting with my agent at eleven. I can just make it, can you call a cab?

Robin gets up quickly and gets dressed. Carl calls the cab. Before he knows it Suzie is about to leave. She kisses him.

ROBIN

Look, I'm here for you, for the future. I think last night may have been a blessing in disguise and we, you and me, we can make something work. But right now I've got to split.

CARL

I love you Robin, I do.

ROBIN

I know, but you've got to sort your shit out right?

CARL

I'm on it.

Robin leaves and Carl gets up. He showers then puts on his paint covered boiler suit, puts some music on and resumes painting another of Suzie's nudes from which he pulls the sheet that is covering it. He stands in front of it for a moment then hears Milan's voice.

                    MILAN (V/O)
Now work! Now work…

In the mess of the aftermath of the party, he paints with a passion and an intensity, and speeded up the painting develops quickly.

INT. CARL'S STUDIO - EVENING

It is night and all the curtains are drawn with just some small lights illuminating Carl's work area as he is still painting. Some music plays from the Hi-Fi. The door buzzer sounds, Carl walks over and opens the door, it's Suzie. She storms in and starts attacking Carl immediately.

                    SUZIE
You think you're so bloody smart. You've got a chip on
your shoulder that says you think everyone else is
beneath you, with your perfect artist lifestyle and your
stupid designer warehouse studio. You're a cliche
Carl!

                    CARL
Hello Suzie.

                    SUZIE
I'm not an empty vessel you know. I have a degree, I
have depth, and I'm... profound, it's just I don't know
how to show it, to anyone.

                    CARL
You're just great Suzie, just as you are.

SUZIE

I don't need you to tell me that. In fact I'm doing just
fine as a matter of fact. What is it with you and Robin
then? You couldn't keep your eyes off her, you were all
over her. You might as well have got down in the
middle of the floor and done it right there and then!

CARL

I'm sorry Suzie, Robin and I go way back, we were
years deep in each others lives, and I, well I hadn't
seen her for a long time.

SUZIE

Ok, Ok, I get it. But what about me, you totally ignored
me all night, and Robin, well Robin just walked right
through me like I wasn't there. I know, I know, she's
amazing and incredible and talented and everything
else that I want to be, or anyone would want to be.

CARL

She's not perfect Suzie, she's pretty scarred inside in
loads of ways really but we understand each other. I,
er, saw you with Martin, did anything...

SUZIE

Martin was a perfect gentleman and took me home in
his car, in his sports car, it's only been through his
kindness that I've made it through the day. We had
lunch.

CARL

Is there anything that I can do, I mean to help.

SUZIE

No, I don't think there is, I just came to get my stuff
and leave this, this big black box that you live in, then
I'll be gone.

CARL

Alright, I'll just be here.

SUZIE

Right then.

Suzie goes to the bedroom and collects a few items of clothing. She
sees the miniature camera and decides to take it too, covering it with
her clothes.

SUZIE

I'm going, don't call me, I won't answer. And by the
way, I never liked your paintings, they're unoriginal
and fake, like you.

CARL

Oh.

Suzie storms off... shouting as she goes.

SUZIE

At least I know what I am!

She exits but leaves the door open. Carl walks over to shut it and sees
Suzie getting into Martin's convertible sports car, which then speeds
away into the night.

CARL

Martin Stevens, what a charlatan.

He shuts the door. Seemingly unaffected he slowly walks back to the painting of Suzie, which she obviously didn't see, and continues painting to the music.

INT. CARL'S STUDIO - DAY

Sebastian is at Carl's and they're playing a two player retro video game with joysticks, projected huge onto the large wall.

> SEBASTIAN
> So quit messing around, tell me, when me and Iris left it was just you, Robin and the Dj.

> CARL
> She stayed, and left the next morning.

> SEBASTIAN
> Is that it, is that all I get?

> CARL
> What else do you want to know?

> SEBASTIAN
> Oh come on, you spend you whole time at college and you both miss out on what could have been the most creative relationship of your lives. Now you finally get it on and you won't even fill your old buddy in on the juicy details!

> CARL
> What makes you think we weren't all sorted at college?

SEBASTIAN

You were!?

CARL

Yeah, we used to go to hotels. It was more fun keeping it quiet.

SEBASTIAN

All that time and not a peep to me.

CARL

Concentrate on the game Seb, you're losing.

SEBASTIAN

And now you're back in the sack, this is monumental stuff!

CARL

I'm not so sure now though, it's the fame thing, she's an actress Seb.

SEBASTIAN

My god, what is your problem with acting?

CARL

She dropped out of college, to become an actress, and she never told me why, she just left me and didn't look back and she never told me why.

SEBASTIAN

Have you asked her?

CARL

No, I'm not sure I want to know. Why does anyone
want to become an actor? Pretending to be someone
they're not, it's a kind of lying don't you think?

SEBASTIAN

Oh grow up dude! It's entertainment, it's a job! Some
people have to work for a living.

CARL

I work.

Sebastian throws down the joystick.

SEBASTIAN

You play. And I've got to admit, you've got quite good
at it. Look, if you bail on Robin now, you're a total
idiot and I'll disown you. Take a chance on her, you
know who she was, you know who she is.

CARL

That's just it, everybody knows who she is.

SEBASTIAN

For fuck's sake, show her who you are!

Carl puts down the joystick, and a change comes across his face. He
looks at Sebastian with a dead pan face and speaks in a monotone
voice.

CARL

I don't think I know who I am Seb. It's a little detail I'm
having real trouble with at the moment. And I don't

think anyone else can help me with it right now. I
think you better go, because I need to work.

Sebastian is in shock, they stay eyes locked for some time until
Sebastian stands up and walks.

> SEBASTIAN
> I'm not sure what kind of trip you're on Carl, but if you
> want me to go, I'll go. Call me if you need me. For
> everyones sake, get your shit sorted.

Sebastian leaves the studio and Carl starts playing the video game
again, pressing ONE PLAYER ONLY.

EXT./INT. MARTIN'S CAR - DAY

Martin is driving Suzie through the countryside in his convertible car.
They shout over the sound of the wind.

> MARTIN
> The director asked if my insurance covered it and I just
> told him, hey, sometimes we just have to do what we
> have to do. So I had to do the stunt myself.

> SUZIE
> Were you ok?

> MARTIN
> No, I broke my stupid leg. But they kept the shot in
> the final edit. It looks very realistic, you should rent it.

> SUZIE
> What was it called again?

                    MARTIN
A Month To Die For, we shot it all on location in Wales.
The Welsh all speak backwards, did you know that?

                    SUZIE
No, no I didn't.

                    MARTIN
Rufus has lined up a screen test for you. I'll be there
too, should be a walk in the park if you're as good as I
think you are.

                    SUZIE
Oh, I'm good alright.

She looks away.

INT. SEBASTIAN'S APARTMENT - DAY

Iris and Sebastian are at work in his study. Iris is working on the pizza
puppet and Sebastian is leafing through some larger storyboards.

                    SEBASTIAN
I think he's losing it, really. He was, odd, I've never
seen him like that before, except for maybe when his
dad passed away.

                    IRIS
What do you think he's going through?

SEBASTIAN

I don't know whether it was Suzie or Robin, whatever but since the exhibition he's, he's missing something, something or someone has got into him.

IRIS

Is he painting?

SEBASTIAN

Yeah, he's painting but he won't tell me what and he doesn't want to talk about it.

IRIS

Do you think he believes in himself, as an artist I mean?

SEBASTIAN

That's it, I don't think he ever has, not since I've known him. He just seems to go through the motions and now he's found some success, the wheels are coming off. The cracks are starting to show, I'm telling you, I'm worried about him.

IRIS

I think maybe he might be happy inside for the first time in a long time and he's forgotten how to show it.

SEBASTIAN

Possibly, it's not easy reading his emotions.

IRIS

Suzie's started acting all strange too. Maybe they've really done a number on each other. She doesn't make any sense, it's like she's talking a foreign language and she's definitely heading somewhere I've never heard of. And here's the thing, she's started sleeping over at Martin Stevens place.

                    SEBASTIAN
Never.

                    IRIS
It's true, she's even got a a key.

                    SEBASTIAN
A key?!

                    IRIS
Yep, a key.

INT. MODERN PUBLIC ART GALLERY - DAY

Robin is walking through a modern art gallery on her own. She's relaxed and carefree, swinging a small bag and stopping at particular paintings that she likes. A YOUNG COUPLE (20s) notice her and walk up to her.

                    YOUNG WOMAN
Er, sorry to bother you. You're Robin Tucker aren't you.

                    ROBIN
Yes, that I am, indeed.

                    YOUNG MAN
We noticed you from over there, and I thought we shouldn't bother you but…

                    YOUNG WOMAN
We're both such big fans, I feel kind of foolish, I expect
this happens to you all the time.

                        ROBIN
Actually not so often, I think people just think I look
like someone they recognise.

                    YOUNG WOMAN
Could we get a selfie?

                        ROBIN
Sure.

They take a selfie with a famous painting for a background.

                     YOUNG MAN
Our friends aren't going to believe this.

                        ROBIN
You've got proof now!

                    YOUNG WOMAN
Can you sign our programme?

                        ROBIN
No, problem.

Robin signs their programme with a pen they give to her.

                    YOUNG WOMAN
You're even nicer in reality than in your movies.

ROBIN

I've done some pretty lousy movies, so I'm not so sure…

YOUNG MAN

We won't take up any more of your time. Thank you so much.

ROBIN

It's my pleasure, really, a perk of the job.

YOUNG WOMAN

Thank you. Thank you. Good bye.

The young couple walk away and Robin smiles to herself before carrying on to look at the exhibits. Other members of the public walk on by unaware of the star in their midst.

INT. SCREEN TEST ROOM - DAY

Suzie is standing in a film studio space, lit by a key light and fill. Rufus Ronson and Martin Stevens sit beside a camera which is manned by a cameraman and a female assistant. There is a sound person and a boom operator and a couple of grips but otherwise the scene is quite close and personal.

RUFUS

Ok Suzie, we'll take it from the beginning of your monologue. Are you ok with that?

SUZIE

Yes, yes that's fine, just a moment.

She checks her script which is on a chair, then replaces it and stands composed.

                    SUZIE
    I'm ready.

                    RUFUS
    Ok. Camera.

                    CAMERA
    Rolling.

                    RUFUS
    Sound.

                    SOUND
    Speed.

                    RUFUS
    Alright, Suzie, when you feel ready.

Suzie relaxes and takes her time for this chance of a lifetime. After a moment she begins her piece, looking directly at Rufus and Roger she uses her whole body to put everything into the performance.

                    SUZIE
    The foul look of his contorted face as though he'd had
    the last laugh. The unnatural way his broken limbs
    were twisted, twisted and gnarly like the roots of a tree.
    No one would shed a tear for him or his like, and I
    couldn't help but wonder if this was his last mark on
    the world he'd left behind. Was his journey over now or
    was he merely handing the baton to me? I already
    knew one of his secrets now I had to carry his legacy

                    91

towards another world, a world where dead men speak and the living have to listen. I'd heard his voice and it had put the chill in me. It was fearful cold running through my very soul and I vowed never to go to that place again.

Suzie stops and comes out of the zone in which she has put herself, back to her normal self, having perfectly executed the piece. After a long pause, Rufus Ronson seems happy.

RUFUS

Cut. That's perfect Suzie. We need to do some serious thinking now. We've got your number. We'll get back to you in a couple of days, no longer.

SUZIE

Thank you so much, I really enjoyed it. Bye Martin.

MARTIN

Bye Suze, later.

Suzie leaves and when she's gone Rufus talks to Martin.

RUFUS

She is good.

MARTIN

She is.

RUFUS

It's a risk though, don't you think?

MARTIN

What did you say at the outset, new talent, new direction.

RUFUS

Robin will be cut up about it. We haven't signed a
contract with her just yet... This girl though, this Suzie
Richards. I think she's made for the big screen and we
get to discover her, cast her in her first feature.

MARTIN

There is something else. I'd like to put in my personal
preference. Me and Suzie, we've been seeing rather a
lot of each other, lately and she, it's hard to say, she
lifts me. And I know I can shape her into what we
need.

RUFUS

That kind of chemistry could work well in this story.

MARTIN

So we're agreed then?

RUFUS

Looks like we've got a new leading lady.

EXT. CASA NUEVA GALLERY - DAY

A large white van pulls up and parks on the double yellow lines outside
the gallery with its warning lights on. Carl jumps out of the passenger
side, quickly followed by JON (36) a young the driver who goes round
the back and opens the van doors. Together they unload and carry a
large bubble wrapped canvass from the van into the gallery, the glass
doors opening as they approach.

INT. CASA NUEVA GALLERY - DAY

Carl and Jon carry the picture into the gallery, and lean it against a wall.
Carl is unshaven and looking a bit unkempt.

                              CARL
           Thanks Jon, that's amazing, I owe you.

                              JON
           No, trouble Carl, I owed you one so I think we're even.

                              CARL
           Cool, see you soon.

                              JON
           Cheers.

Jon leaves the gallery, gets in his van and drives away. Chloe walks
from the back of the gallery, followed soon after by Milan.

                              CHLOE
           Carl darling, so good to see you. I see you've been
           busy. What do you have for me.

                              CARL
           This is the first in a series.

He begins to unwrap the painting, Its is revealed a little at a time and
then in full.

                              CHLOE
           Oh.

CARL

What do you think?

CHLOE

It's very, bare. Wait a moment, is that you I think it is?
It looks remarkably like our young Suzie.

CARL

She was the model, yes.

CHLOE

I'm really not sure Carl my boy, it's rather a departure
from your previous works, the ones that sold so well.

CARL

You wanted different, you wanted authentic, original.

Carl has a note of desperation in his voice.

CHLOE

Yes, but our clients are looking for something a deeper,
more profound, a little more subtle and… abstract.

Carl is at a loss for words.

MILAN

I like it, it has a certain honesty a kind of innocent
freedom.

CHLOE

I'm not sure I can take it my love.

MILAN

Take it Chloe. Carl, do you have any more?

CARL

Yes, there's about fifteen in the series. This is the best I've done, this is the best I can do.

Carl is in disbelief.

CHLOE

Ok, I'll display it for a limited time, we might get lucky.

MILAN

If it sells, I'd be more than happy to look at the rest. I think these could do well in my little Amsterdam shop.

CARL

Ok, we're ok then.

Carl take some breaths and calms down.

CARL

Good. Is Suzie here? I wanted to talk with her if that's possible.

CHLOE

Suzie has gone. She left a few days ago with some ridiculous excuse about acting and a movie and wot not. Why don't you take a break from painting for a while my love, think about something else for a while, take a holiday from yourself.

CARL

That's perhaps the best idea I've heard for a very long time. Can I go home now then?

MILAN

Yes, you can go home. Have you answered the
question?

Milan has somehow moved closer to Carl and is talking to him softly in
a deep whisper again.

MILAN

You can go home now...

Carl moves away.

CARL

I'm going home now. Bye Bye.

Chloe and Milan wave as he turns and leaves.

INT. SUZIE AND IRIS' APARTMENT - NIGHT

Iris is sitting watching the tv, a cartoon is playing. Suzie comes out of
her bedroom with great energy.

SUZIE

Iris this can't go on anymore, I have to tell you, I'm
about to burst!

IRIS

What do you mean?

SUZIE

I'm packing up and I'm moving out to live with Martin
permanently. I have the leading female role in Rufus

Ronson's new independent noir thriller opposite Martin and I'm going to be famous.

IRIS

I'm happy for you Suzie, I am, it's what you've wanted for, well at least three months now.

SUZIE

It's no use trying to talk me out of it, I've made my mind up and I'm acting on it.

IRIS

Go for it, knock 'em dead.

SUZIE

You don't have anything else to say?

IRIS

Look Suze, it's your life but I've got to say you don't have to go around being 'in character' the whole time.

SUZIE

I'm sure I don't know what you mean.

IRIS

Take a break, or you'll find yourself living in a funny little bubble that you won't be able to break out of.

SUZIE

Is that it?

IRIS

I have some news too, I'm moving in with Sebastian. I guess this little apartment will be the location for some other people's story in a very short while.

SUZIE

Congratulations, I think. You should follow your dreams. I know the world of puppets means a lot to you but if you want my advice, puppets will only get you so far, one day you're going to have to grow up and be a real person.

IRIS

Hey! Puppets have feelings too you know!

SUZIE

Oh, you're impossible!

Suzie storms back into her bedroom to finish her packing.

INT. CARL'S STUDIO - NIGHT

Carl breaks down alone. With music playing, he stands in the large space in the middle of his studio and taking a large pot of white emulsion paint, he begins to pour a trail of paint on the floor around himself. Starting from the outside he makes an ever tightening spiral perhaps twenty feet across, around and around, getting smaller and smaller, until he is left standing at it's centre. He throws the nearly empty pot of paint away from himself, half-way across the studio, then he sits down in the middle of the spiral, puts his head in his hands and cries.

INT. ROBIN'S AGENT'S OFFICE - DAY

Robin is in her agent's office, once more sitting across from Charlie.
She sits with a look of disbelief and shock.

> CHARLIE
> I'm afraid that's it Robin. They made their minds up
> before the contracts were signed. I know it sucks.
> They've chosen some new girl, untried talent, someone
> by the name of... Suzie Richards, I've never heard of
> her.

There is a long pause.

> ROBIN
> I have. I bet Martin Stevens had his grubby little hands
> all over this. I don't believe it, this was going to be my
> vehicle to the USA. I would have had my pick over
> there.

> CHARLIE
> Is that what you really want?

> ROBIN
> It's the natural progression, don't you think?

> CHARLIE
> It doesn't have to be. You go to American you'd be lost
> in a sea of all those hopeful young wannabes, and
> before you know it you'd be in some action flick, or
> some gross out comedy.

100

                              ROBIN

I just want to do quality work, I really do. Maybe I've
just become distracted by the Ronson machine.

                             CHARLIE

He does make very successful movies Robin and the
chances are this one will do just as well, but you have
to let go of it, and there are alternatives.

                              ROBIN

What are my alternatives?

                             CHARLIE

OK.

Charlie picks up a script and hands it to Robin.

                             CHARLIE

This is shooting in the Czech Republic in just a few
months. There's a part in it, a femme fatale in fact, you
would be perfect for it, I think it's a real opportunity.

Robin takes the script.

                              ROBIN

Who's the director?

                             CHARLIE

It's Frederic Silberzan. He's well into his 70s now, I
know, but apparently he believes this is his
masterpiece, maybe even his swan-song.

                               101

                    ROBIN
Phew... Silberzan, he was a bit good in the early 80s,
some really classy art-house cinema. I thought he'd
retired.

                    CHARLIE
Well, he's back, and he's specifically asked for you...

Robin looks up from scanning through the script and Charlie smiles.

INT. CARL'S STUDIO - NIGHT

The door to the studio is open. Sebastian comes in and calls out.

                    SEBASTIAN
    Carl!

Carl appears from the kitchen carrying a pot plant and a cup of coffee.
His beard has grown and his boiler suit is covered in paint. He is
subdued.

                    CARL
Heh Seb, how are you, do you want a coffee?

He offers his own mug towards Sebastian.

                    SEBASTIAN
No, I'm fine, you have it.

Sebastian walks further in at the studio which hasn't even been cleaned
up since the party. There is a lot of mess everywhere. In particular he
looks at the paint spiral on the floor, which dominates the place.
Sebastian is gentle.

                    102

SEBASTIAN

What's going on here, buddy?

CARL

Oh, I guess you'd call that... performance art of some
sort, or maybe an installation. It's order out of chaos.

SEBASTIAN

Looks like you might need to do a little spring cleaning
in here sometime. Maybe we should just sit down for a
bit, how do you feel about that?

CARL

Sounds fine.

Sebastian clears away some rubbish and they sit down next to each
other on one of the large leather sofas.

SEBASTIAN

What's on your mind? You can talk about it if you like.

CARL

Oh, not much.

SEBASTIAN

You've got that crazy look going on.

CARL

Yeah, there's a bit of madness in there somewhere.
Seb, tell me... how would you define originality?

SEBASTIAN

It's something, unique, something that's never been
done before.

CARL

Nothing's really original then.

SEBASTIAN

Nothing except who you are inside.

CARL

Yeah, well I'm having trouble with that. I'm formulaic, derivative, unoriginal, shallow, unauthentic and lacking in integrity.

Sebastian suddenly snaps out of this conversation.

SEBASTIAN

Shit man! We went through stuff like this when you're dad died, when Robin disappeared. I'm not going through it all again. Yes, you're going through something now but you've got to make a stand. You know, I have to say this, the best advice I can give to you right now is to get some kind of job.

CARL

Isn't all this a job?

He waves his arms around the studio.

SEBASTIAN

No, no it isn't. I can't lie to you. At best what you've got here is some kind of, business, for want of a better word and by the looks of things you're not really doing any business at all.

                    CARL
I've got ideas. I just have to go back to the start. Can
you go away now Seb, I think it's best if I clean up.

                  SEBASTIAN
I can help if you like?

                    CARL
No, you've got to tidy up your own mess.

                  SEBASTIAN
You'll be alright?

                    CARL
Yeah, I'll be fine. Don't worry Seb, I'll call you when...
I'll call you.

INT. SEBASTIAN'S CAR - DAY

Sebastian gets in his car and immediately calls Robin.

                  SEBASTIAN
Hi, Robin, it's Seb, have you got a minute, it's about
Carl.

INT. ROBIN'S APARTMENT - DAY

Robin is in her kitchen making some food and now talking on the
phone.

                    ROBIN
Hi, See, what's up? What is it, you sound stressed.

SEBASTIAN

It's Carl, he's losing it, or he's lost it, I'm not sure
which.

ROBIN

May be it's been a long time coming, maybe it's a good
thing.

SEBASTIAN

It's not a good thing! The guys living in his own shit.
I'm really worried about him. I just saw him.

ROBIN

What was he doing?

SEBASTIAN

He wasn't doing anything. Can you call him? I think
you might be able to reach him.

There is a long pause.

SEBASTIAN

Robin? Are you there?

ROBIN

I'm here. He needs to call me, he needs to come to me.

SEBASTIAN

Look now's not the time for playing games Robin.

ROBIN

It's the only way forward for him, the only way he's
going to fix himself. He needs to find what he needs to
come to me. Trust me Seb, I know he's your friend but

106

I know him. He'll call when he's ready and when he's
ready I'll be here for him.

                    SEBASTIAN
Ok, Ok, I get you. I just want him back to his self.

                    ROBIN
He's just trying to find out who that is, that's all.

INT. LONDON BAR - NIGHT

Robin is having drinks with JOSH (35), a financial type in a quiet bar
which is beautifully lit and tastefully decorated. The two are close and
seem to be getting closer.

                    JOSH
I imagine all the guys in your life just want to be with
you because you're famous right?

                    ROBIN
Not all of them, but yes, I get that a lot.

                    JOSH
You see with me, you've got someone from another
world. It's funny, futures and commodities are probably
so alien to you but to me they are bread and butter,
meat and potatoes.

                    ROBIN
I must say I'm always interested in discovering the
details of the lives of other microcosms. My life on the
other hand is an open book, you see my films, you see
me, what you see is what you get.

JOSH

There's no knowing how people's work life impacts on their private life but I feel with you, I already know you somewhat, perhaps because you put your own character into your film.

ROBIN

Ah, you'll find there's at least two of me, on screen and off, but to some extent you're right. All these little gestures and mannerisms you see in the films have to come from somewhere.

JOSH

May I ask you a personal question Robin? Do you already have a stockbroker to manage your financial portfolio?

INT. CARL'S STUDIO - DAY

The studio is back to its functional and tidy state. Carl is just finishing off removing the paint from the floor. He looks around takes a deep breath and calls Robin.

CARL

Hi, Robin, it's Carl. Yeah I'm good. Listen can we meet? How about by that bench in the park where we used to always go. Now would be good, if you're free. Cool, I'll be there in say, an hour. See you then.

He hangs up.

> CARL (To himself)

That wasn't so hard. I think I need a shower, a shave and some clean clothes.

EXT. PARK - DAY

Carl is sitting on an isolated bench in a beautiful park. There are cyclists, dog-walkers, and people walking by every now and then. Some kids are playing with a frisbee nearby and the sun is shining. Robin walks up to him.

> ROBIN

Hello stranger.

> CARL

Oh, it's a beautiful... random actress. Take a seat.

Robin sits down.

> ROBIN

Are you OK? Seb rang, he was pretty worried about you.

> CARL

Yeah, I'm fine, really. I was just going through one. You know how it is, the artistic search for meaning.

> ROBIN

I do know how that is. What are we doing here Carl? Where do we go from here?

Carl looks around at the beauty of the surroundings.

CARL

It's lovely here isn't?

ROBIN

It is, it really is.

CARL

I've got a question I have to ask you Robin. I just want
a straight answer. I don't know if it means much but
it's been on my mind.

ROBIN

So, what is it, what's the question?

CARL

Why did you decide to become an actress?

Robin takes a deep sigh.

ROBIN

I had no alternative. All that work we did at college, I
kept asking myself, who am I? And I gained, self
knowledge. I learned about myself and learned what I
was. I realised I was someone who acts. I couldn't
change that any more than I could change being a
person. Being an actor and being a person become one
and the same thing. Does that make any sense?

CARL

It does. So I've got one more question, then I promise
I'm done. How would you *define* an actor?

                              ROBIN

          People will tell you all kinds of things but for me... It's
          just someone who knows how to change.

                              CARL

          You make it sound easy.

                              ROBIN

          It is easy, or at least it can be natural. But I suppose
          there is something else... An actor is someone who
          needs guidance, reassurance and someone they can
          trust to catch them when they fall.

                              CARL

          We like each other Robin, and I think we need each
          other. You can trust me.

                              ROBIN

          I do.

They put there arms around each other and kiss. In the middle of their
embrace the kids' frisbee lands on their feet. The kids laugh and Robin
and Carl laugh too. Carl throws the frisbee back.

                              CARL

          Come on, let's walk. I realised on the way here, I just
          need a new role to play.

They get up off the bench and walk.

                              ROBIN

          Let me write it for you.

                          CARL

   OK.

As they walk away, Carl has his arm around Robin's shoulder and she
has put her hand in his back jeans' pocket.

INT. CLOTHES SHOP - DAY

Iris and Robin are in a high street clothes shop, looking through all
kinds of clothes, as they choose clothes and look at them in a mirror as
they talk. Robin holds up a dress.

                          ROBIN
   This would look nice on you.

                          IRIS
   Nah, not my colour. I don't dress like a puppet you
   know.

                          ROBIN
   Oh, OK. How did you get into puppets anyway.

                          IRIS
   You get to try it out one day and then you get hooked.
   It's the power, the control, it's addictive.

                          ROBIN
   Have you been doing it long?

                          IRIS
   About five years now. Of course it becomes a way of
   life. You know the best thing about puppets though?

ROBIN

No.

IRIS

You're invisible. I know, it sounds insane but you do
your thing, and nobody knows you're doing it.
Anonymity combined with power and control, you
can't beat it.

ROBIN

That's very cool.

IRIS

I know. Heh, but there's one thing I was going to ask
you. I've watched your films now and it's like you've
got no strings attached. I totally independently
motivated, self-propelled and self-contained. So I just
have to ask, to get it out the way, you're not a robot are
you?

Robin laughs.

ROBIN

No, I'm not a robot. There's a director he or she tells
you what to do, then you do it in your own way.

IRIS

Ah yeah, a director. They must be like the puppet
master. And while we're at it, falling in love in a
movie, is that any different from falling in love for
real?

                    ROBIN

I don't want to burst your bubble but people don't fall
in love in the movies.

                    IRIS

Of course they do! I've seen it hundreds of times!
Really and you call yourself an actress.

Robin is smiling.

                    ROBIN

How are you and Sebastian working out together.

                    IRIS

Oh, fine, just fine. He's a bit stupid but he's rich and
kind and they're the two most important things. Oh
I've go to ask you would you and Carl like to come to
lunch at our place on Saturday?

                    ROBIN

Yes, that would be lovely.

                    IRIS

We should have a bit of a surprise for you both. How
about this jumper for you?

Iris holds up a bright orange jumper and Robin shakes her head.

EXT. CHELSEA, STREET -DAY

Suzie and Martin walk along the street nearby the gallery. They look as
if they are in disguise wearing 'movie' clothes and sporting sunglasses.

SUZIE

Would you like to see where I use to work?

MARTIN

Sure, lead the way.

They walk a little further, cross the road and arrive in front of the gallery. In the window Carl's large nude of Suzie is on display. Suzie takes off her sunglasses.

SUZIE

Now that is good.

MARTIN

Look Carl Lloyd-Brooks, it's one of Carl's. In fact…

Martin tilts his head.

MARTIN

…that looks remarkably like you Suzie.

SUZIE

It is me. I was a model for a while.

MARTIN

I wonder how much they are asking for it. I feel a purchase coming along. Let's go in.

They walk into the gallery.

EXT. THE SOUTH BANK - DAY

Carl is walking along the riverside with his camera taking street photographs. He's relaxed and enjoying both the sunshine and his freedom. He makes his shots of many different subjects and every time he takes a picture the photograph is shown, sometimes in black and white, sometimes in colour. His photographs are candid capturing people of all ages and types. He sits down and takes pictures from waist level within this vibrant city scene.

EXT. LONDON STREET - DAY

Suzie is now walking on her own, she turns a corner and bumps into Robin.

                    SUZIE
        Robin!

                    ROBIN
        Suzie! Fancy this, I'd been sort of hoping I'd bump
        into you, and sort of hoping I wouldn't too.

                    SUZIE
        Perhaps we have a few things we need to talk about.

                    ROBIN
        Mmm... What about a coffee? There's a cafe just
        there.

                    SUZIE
        Certainly, but I can't be long. I have some
        commitments.

                    ROBIN
    I'm sure you do. Let's go.

They walk.

INT. CAFE - DAY

Robin and Suzie sit at a window seat next to each other. The mood is
tense and they both talk in a controlled professional manner.

                    SUZIE
    Look, the first thing I have to say is that I'm sorry I
    took your place in the Ronson film, but you did steal
    my boyfriend.

                    ROBIN
    Just think of it as me reclaiming him from lost and
    found after rather a lengthy absence.

                    SUZIE
    I can live with that. Any how I'm with Martin now,
    we're very happy.

                    ROBIN
    Maybe we're both just a couple of thieves, maybe
    we've both got just what we wanted. How's the filming
    going?

                    SUZIE
    We start tomorrow.

                    ROBIN
You've got a lot of hard work ahead of you, are you
sure you can handle it?

                    SUZIE
Rufus is a very kind and talented man, I'm sure he'll
give me plenty of guidance and I've got Martin for
support, I'm sure I'll manage.

                    ROBIN
Let me give you some words of wisdom Suzie, from
experience. First Rufus will do whatever it takes to
squeeze every living emotion out of your soul in
service of the story. For him the story is all that he
cares about and he will make you do anything he wants
in service of the story. You are now his plaything.
Second, Martin will do precisely what Rufus tells him
to, no matter how base or repulsive in behaviour. So
long as you know this you'll be prepared, for tomorrow.

Suzie looks genuinely concerned and becomes visibly vulnerable.

                    SUZIE
How do you suggest I best approach this?

                    ROBIN
Grin and bear it. Take whatever they throw and you
and throw it back twice as hard. And if you can't
handle it, make yourself as big as you can, and exit the
whole damn thing. That's all I can say. I've got to go.

Robin stands and leaves.

SUZIE

Thank you.

ROBIN

Good luck!

INT. SEBASTIAN'S APARTMENT - NIGHT

Robin and Carl, both casually dressed visit Sebastian and Iris for dinner. They are sitting at the table, having just finished eating and are drinking wine, and laughing.

CARL

There's something I've got to say.

SEBASTIAN

Just say it then!

CARL

I know you guys have been worried about me lately but everything's cool, or getting cooler anyway. The thing is... I've quit painting, I'm just not going to do it anymore, AND I'm leaving the Studio to move in with Robin. That's it, that's what I had to say.

SEBASTIAN

That might be just about the biggest thing you've ever said and I'm totally with you my friend. But I've got to ask, what are you going to do instead?

CARL

I'm going to do something with my photography, I'm not sure what yet, I mean it was what I originally went

to college to study, before I got distracted!
Photography is the way to go, I've got faith in it.

Robin, takes his hand.

IRIS
If it doesn't work out you can help me make puppets, I
was thinking of doing one of Seb, but I thought it
might be a bit creepy. What do you think?

ROBIN
No, definitely do it, then we can all take turns
controlling him, making him do anything and
everything we want. Is it like a voodoo doll?

IRIS
Of course, that's the whole philosophy of puppets.

SEBASTIAN
Oh, there's a philosophy now! I think it's time we did
the big reveal, what do you think Iris?

IRIS
Roll tape!

SEBASTIAN
I hope you're ready for this.

Sebastian takes a remote control and turns on a large wall mounted tv
screen, he presses 'play' and a test card comes up which is shortly
followed by the pizza commercial. "Puppetelli's Pizza" bursts onto the
screen. There is a Puppet on strings talking to camera whilst another
puppet makes a pizza on the table next to him.

PUPPETELLI PUPPET

At Puppetelli's Pizza we don't lie about the quality of our Pizza. Delicious, rich, full flavoured stone baked Pizza pies. Guaranteed you won't be disappointed when you open the box. Twice the topping, double thickness crust and two opportunities to bag a bargain. Two for the price of one on Tuesdays and Thursdays and if you buy two at the weekend you'll get a third free! With double fast delivery you'll be doubly happy. Pinocchio Pizza, don't let other companies string you along!

It's over very quickly and everyone is in a state of shock. Iris and Sebastian look on in hope.

ROBIN

You did all that!

SEBASTIAN

Team effort.

CARL

It's the best thing I've ever seen. I want to order a Puppetelli now!

ROBIN

It's amazing, I can't, I'm speechless.

SEBASTIAN

Goes live on all major commercial channels in a week.

IRIS

And the best thing is we get to watch it every day for a couple of months!

121

ROBIN

I give up, as an actor I am now officially redundant.
Puppets will take over the world and it will be a far
better place for it!

They drink and carry on talking into the night.

EXT. LONDON CITY SKY LINE - NIGHT

With the moon hanging over the city, lights in houses, high rise
buildings and cars on the roads, mark the passing of another night.

EXT. RONSON MOVIE LOCATION SHOOT - DAY

Set to music the scene is of a small crew gathered around Rufus
Ronson, Suzie and Martin as they go for another take on the first day of
shooting. Suzie is highly agitated and Martin is laughing at her. In the
scene Martin has to slap her and Ronson is doing take after take of this
denigrating shot. Every time the sound of the clapper board shuts it is
quickly followed by the sound and image of another slap. It happens
again and again. Finally Suzie has enough. She pushes Martin away
from her, throwing things and knocking down lights as she does. She is
in a rage, shouting and swearing and pushes Rufus Ronson over as she
storms off the location.

INT. CARL'S STUDIO - MORNING

Robin and Carl are in bed in the late morning, awake, sitting up and
drinking coffee.

                    ROBIN

You're not going to miss all this are you?

                    CARL

All what?

                    ROBIN

All this, the studio…

                    CARL

Nah, I'm tired of it. Plus it's a bit too big for one, two
big for ten really. I just rattle around in here. Someone
else can make something with it.

                    ROBIN

We're going to have to get going packing stuff up, what
are you going to do with the sofas?

                    CARL

I spoke to the landlord, he said I could leave them here,
in case a new tenant wants them, sell them. If not we
can move them later.

                    ROBIN

What about all your paintings?

                    CARL

I was thinking of having a bonfire, you know just
chuck 'em on.

                    ROBIN

You can't do that!

                    123

CARL

No, I got a call from Milan, he's bought the lot. The one in the gallery sold and all he wanted to know was that they were of a similar subject and quality. He hasn't given me a price yet but he's coming tomorrow to pick them up.

ROBIN

That's great! Some extra Cash!

CARL

He's taking them all to Amsterdam, says I'll be 'Big in Europe'!

ROBIN

Before you pack up all your paints, I was thinking I might paint a picture.

CARL

Wow, really?

ROBIN

It's daft, I haven't so much as lifted a brush since college. I want to see if I've still got what it takes.

CARL

You were always super abstract woman, what are you going to paint?

ROBIN

I've got this, freeze-frame image from a sort of fantasy film in my head, I want to get it out. It'll be like a single frame of film.

CARL

Go for it, we've got a week to get out of here.

ROBIN

That should be plenty of time.

CARL

I've got a few made-up canvasses left. You can choose
one.

ROBIN

Nice!

They drink their coffee.

INT. MARTIN'S BEDROOM - NIGHT

Suzie is lying in Martin's large double bed alone and naked. When
Martin enters the house and the room, he is surprised to find her.

SUZIE

I let myself in. I'm here to say sorry for today.

MARTIN

It was very unprofessional. I'm sorry too, sorry that
you're not on the film anymore. Rufus has already
recast.

SUZIE

I don't care about Rufus, I never did. I just want to
make it up to you. I'd hate to say goodbye to you
without a proper send off.

125

MARTIN

Are you saying what I think you're saying?

SUZIE

Come on in, it's lovely and warm in here.

Martin takes his clothes off and gets into bed. After only a short while of kissing, Suzie, seductively ties his wrists and ankles to the four corners of the bed.

MARTIN

Hey I'm not so sure about all this.

SUZIE

It's a trust thing, no risk no reward.

Martin is now fully tied up. Suzie gets off the bed with Martin completely immobilised and naked. She gets dressed quickly.

SUZIE

Look up.

Martin looks up at the nude painting of her by Carl, which he has had placed on the ceiling.

SUZIE

That's art, this is the real thing. Don't' confuse the two.

She then takes the mini camera she stole from Carl and takes a photograph of him.

SUZIE

And that's going to be art too. Maybe it's art for art's sake, but it's art all the same. Someone will probably find you in a few days. Ciao!

Suzie leaves the room and the house.

EXT. CARL'S STUDIO - DAY

Milan helps Carl move all his wrapped up paintings out of the studio and into his van which is parked outside. They carry the last one out of the studio, down the fire escape and towards the van.

MILAN

So we're agreed, five hundred a piece.

CARL

Sounds good to me.

MILAN

Seems a shame to be getting out of the art game just when you're finding success.

CARL

That just depends on your definition of success doesn't it.

MILAN

Robin is a well known actress isn't she?

CARL

Yes, she is.

MILAN

Very versatile, your modern actress. One minute
they're jumping over a car, then they're in a fist fight,
next thing they're saving the world, then they're in-
between the sheets with someone from another planet!

CARL

Just like real life.

MILAN

Exactly. The thing is there's thousand of actors out
there, at any one time. For all we know they may just
be going around making stuff up, acting, in their every
day lives too. Just mixing with unsuspecting normal
folk making up stories on a whim however they feel
like.

CARL

Just like real people.

MILAN

Exactly.

They have placed the painting on top of the large pile of others in the
back of the van and Milan closes the door.

MILAN

Well, young man, that's us. I wish you well with your
future, however it pans out. Ciao now!

Milan walks away and gets into his van.

CARL

Cheers Milan, all the best.

Milan drives away, waving out the window and beeps his horn. As Carl walks back to the studio he hears Milan's voice in his mind.

                    MILAN (V/O)
        Who is Carl Lloyd-Brooks?

Carl shakes his head and laughs.

INT. CARL'S STUDIO - DAY

Robin and Carl are packing stuff up into boxes. Suzie walks through the open door.

                    SUZIE
        Hello!

Robin and Carl stop what they're doing and walk over to her. She stands in the same clothes as when we first saw her, elegant and simple.

                    CARL
        Hi Suzie, how are you doing?

                    SUZIE
        Sorry to intrude, I just wanted to drop by to say Hi and
        goodbye too.

                    ROBIN
        How's the filming going, have you got a spare day off?

                    SUZIE
        No, no, I quit the film, I just walked away. It wasn't
        what I was expecting it to be. You were right, I'm just
        not built for it.

ROBIN

You know it's probably for the best. It's not for
everyone.

SUZIE

I realise that, I've quit the whole acting thing too, it just
isn't me, literally speaking.

CARL

What about Martin? What did he have to say about the
whole thing?

SUZIE

He was part of the problem as a matter of fact, he
wasn't... treating me appropriately, when I was with
him alone or on the set. And when he was with
Ronson, he just became another animal. It's like he
has two alter egos, each as bad as the other.

CARL

Yeah, he's a dog alright. I hope he gets what's coming
to him.

SUZIE

It's funny you should say that because I've sort of taken
care of that. I can't talk about it right now.

ROBIN

Some actors are in it for all the wrong reasons. The
scary thing is they usually get quite successful by it.

SUZIE

I wasn't happy as an actress I felt I was trapped living
out other people's lives in other people's stories. Iris

said I was staying in character all the time, and that's just a horrible way to live. It's good to feel 'normal' again and know the difference between performing and just being.

ROBIN

Then you *are* a good actress.

CARL

You know Iris has left your flat, she's moved in with Seb. I was just thinking have you got somewhere to go. You can stay here for a while if you need to but I'm moving out in just a few days now.

ROBIN

It would't be a problem, we can make up a bed.

SUZIE

Thank you but no. I feel pretty stupid really, not so long ago I had a great paid regular job, you don't realise how good that is until you lose it, or throw it away for chasing a silly dream.

CARL

Sometimes dreams get a hold of you and lead you round and round in circles 'til you just get dizzy.

ROBIN

Where are you going to stay?

SUZIE

Oh, it's ok. I'm going to do a bit of travelling. I'm going to see my brother in Australia. I've always wanted to visit him. I'll be on a plane this time tomorrow. I'm in a hotel tonight, I haven't got much stuff. There's one thing I want though Carl.

CARL

Whatever it is.

SUZIE

I didn't exactly appreciate you displaying my naked form in the gallery's window. What happened isMartin bought it and put it on the ceiling above the bed in his bedroom. It wouldn't have been so bad except he kept saying how cool it was that he had one of your paintings to look at in bed. He didn't once comment on me. However, I would like you to give me the you took that morning, if you have them.

CARL

Sure, they're just over here.

Carl gets his camera bag and removes a memory card which he hands to Suzie.

CARL

I'm sorry if these caused you trouble.

SUZIE

For what it's worth I think the painting's the best I've seen you do and that morning it was a good memory for me. I'd better go, leave you two in peace. I want to thank you both for letting me into your lives for a short while. Good bye.

She turns and leaves.

                    CARL
        Bye, Suzie. Have a great holiday.

                    ROBIN
        Don't let the bastards grind you down!

Suzie doesn't look back and disappears through the door. Robin and
Carl are left standing for quite a while, speechless and a bit numb.

                    CARL
        She's a good one. Hope she has positive time in
        Australia.

                    ROBIN
        I need to let you know something about my travel
        plans actually.

                    CARL
        I'm ready for anything after that.

                    ROBIN
        I've got this part, it's in a film that shoots in the Czech
        Republic, in a couple of months.

                    CARL
        That's great news!

                    ROBIN
        I wasn't sure how you'd take it. I'll be away for three
        months.

                    CARL
        It's just something I'm going to have to get used to. An
        actor is someone who knows how to change. Maybe I'll

come and visit you on location, make a real nuisance of myself.

                    ROBIN
I'd be happy with that.

                    CARL
I could take a few photographs.

                    ROBIN
I've been meaning to talk to you about that, I had an idea....

INT. AIRPORT - NIGHT

With a stylish new haircut and a completely different look, Suzie makes her way through an airport, dressed for fun, adventure and glamour with the small camera she stole from Carl thrown over her shoulder.

                 CARL (V/O)
Maybe we all just need a change in life every now and then. Things tend to get a little monotonous if you make yourself do the same thing, day after day, over and over again, year in year out. That goes for stacking shelves in a supermarket as well as painting highly saleable but formulaic paintings. Suzie was just bored of who she'd become and wanted only for a change in attitude and a new direction in life and a new look. I think she'll find that, even if she has to go as far away as the other side of the planet.

INT. MARTIN'S BEDROOM - DAY

Martin is still lying naked and tied up to his bed as he looks up to the
nude painting of Suzie.

                    CARL (V/O)
          I never heard from Martin again, and I never called
          him myself. I hope he likes the painting and looks at it
          often, that's all a painter wants really, someone to look
          at there work for a few minutes every day. There was
          an unfortunate picture of him which appeared in the
          more popular press. He was tied to a bed in only his Y-
          Fronts, I always wondered if Suzie had anything to do
          with that. I think the caption read "Sex Slave Stevens".
          It was a rather well written article about the darker side
          the industry.

EXT. SKYDIVING - DAY

Sebastian and Iris are skydiving holding a large banner with the advert
for the pizza company written on it.

                    CARL (V/O)
          Seb's still living it up, the pizza campaign took off but
          Iris has him doing things that he might not have done
          off his own back. She really knows how to pull his
          strings. Life with 'no strings attached' means that one
          has to make ones own moves and trust that there's
          going to be someone there to catch you when you fall.

EXT. AMSTERDAM -DAY

Milan and Chloe are riding through the streets on a tandem bicycle.
Milan is steering, Chloe is on the back.

> ### CARL (V/O)
> Milan and Chloe, well, they're still perched right at the
> top of the highest pinnacle of good taste. I think
> Amsterdam is the perfect place for my career as an
> artist to come to an end. I always wondering what the
> two of them got up to when they weren't wheeling and
> dealing, probably enjoying the finer things in life.

> ### CHLOE
> Yes I know Milan, but is it Art?

INT. CARL'S STUDIO - DAY

Robin has nearly finished painting a widescreen 'freeze frame' picture
of a shot from an imaginary film. It is large and detailed with a
cinematic composition and in this area she is clearly an artist in many
ways too. Carl helps Robin read through and rehearse her Czech
screenplay.

> ### CARL (V/O)
> Robin and I are getting on famously, she finished her
> painting and I've got to say it's pretty good, that's an
> objective opinion from an ex-painter. We've been
> reading through her script for her new movie. I never
> realised how dedicated and professional she is before.
> There's a lot of things I never realised about her before
> but I'm having a lot of fun finding out.

EXT. LONDON PUBLIC SPACES - DAY

Carl is out and about in London with his camera, as at the beginning. There is a long slow zoom in from a very high place until Carl is in close up.

CARL (V/O)
As for me I finally answered the question "Who is Carl Lloyd Brooks?" He's just one of the many people in the credits at the end of a movie. Robin gave me a contact at a production company and they've taken me on as a stills photographer. It's a great job and I get paid! I'm working all the time as a locations scout mainly which is fine because I know this city like the back of my hand. All I have to do is find cool, moody places for film locations, photograph them and send in my shots. And the best bit is I also get to photograph the film shoots themselves. It's great spying on the actors and catching them unawares. The thing is with them you never know when they're acting and when they're just being themselves.

He takes a photograph straight into camera and smiles. The camera swoops up and away.

THE END

If you have enjoyed this book, please leave an interesting review through your Amazon account. Just go to "Your Orders," find this book on your list and then click on "Write A Product Review." This creative feedback not only helps further sales, but also provides valuable information to illustrate the quality and content of ongoing and future work.

Thank you,

Brett Walpole

2020

Printed in Poland
by Amazon Fulfillment
Poland Sp. z o.o., Wrocław

53406150R00083